CONCORDIA LUTHERAN SCHOOL
4663 Lancaster Drive NE
Salem, Oregon 97305
503/393-7188

Dusty's Beary Tales

Building Character
from Bible Virtues

Ruthann Winans and Linda Lee
Illustrations by Mara Mattia

Harvest House Publishers
Eugene, Oregon 97402

Songs used in this book:
Reverend Johnson Oatman, Jr. (words) and Edwin O. Excell (music), "Count Your Blessings," 1897.
Author Unknown, "Tell Me Why the Stars Do Shine."
Joseph Scriven (words), 1857, and Charles C. Converse (music), 1868, "What a Friend We Have in Jesus."

Dusty's Beary Tales

Copyright © 1996 by Ruthann Winans and Linda Lee
Illustrations copyright © 1996 by Mara Mattia
Published by Harvest House Publishers
Eugene, Oregon 97402

Library of Congress Cataloging-in-Publication Data
Winans, Ruthann,
      Dusty's Beary Tales / Ruthann Winans and Linda Lee:
illustrations by Mara Mattia.
      p.   cm.
      Summary: Dusty the bear cub lives with his family in Honey Pine Woods where he learns the values of working together, helping others, trusting in God, and more.

      ISBN 1-56507-496-3 (alk. paper)
      [1. Bears—Fiction. 2. Family life—fiction. 3. Christian life—fiction.] I. Lee, Linda, 1958-   . II. Mattia, Mara, 1952-   . ill. III. Title.
      PZ7.W714Du 1996
      [Fic]—dc20

96-5578
CIP
AC

Printed in the United States of America.

96 97 98 99 00 01 02 03 04 05 / QK / 10 9 8 7 6 5 4 3 2 1

To my wonderful husband, Gary, for embarking with me on life's most exciting adventure . . . Parenthood! And to my three great kids, Dustin Mark, Ashley Ann, and Jason James—you are the treasures of my heart!

RUTHANN WINANS

To my loving husband, Jonathan, for his encouragement. To my terrific daughters, Brianne and Heather, for their endless inspiration. To my baby Jared for his cheerful smiles and giggles. To Grandma Naomi, who generously gaveof her time so that I would have time to write. And to the rest of my treasured family and friends for their support.

My life is truly blessed because of each one of you.

LINDA LEE

To God be the glory! You gave me the gift of my wonderful husband, David, and our three active children, Alan, Janna, and Lisa— who make us old and keep us young!

Thank You for guiding me in spite of myself!

MARA MATTIA

And our special thanks to everyone at Harvest House for making our dream a reality.

RUTHANN, LINDA, MARA

DUSTY'S FAMILY

Papa Boone

Mama Violet

Dusty

Ashley

JJ

Grandpa Buzz

Granny Rose

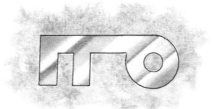

Can you find the key hidden on the cover? The main picture in each chapter also has a key hidden in it. Once you find the key, look for the "Key Thought." The "Key Thought" gives you the key to an important lesson in the story.
Happy hunting!

LET'S START AT THE BEARY BEGINNING

KEY THOUGHT

Look for the hidden key! Then unlock the secret of Honey Pine Woods.
Discover how Beary Tales first came to be.

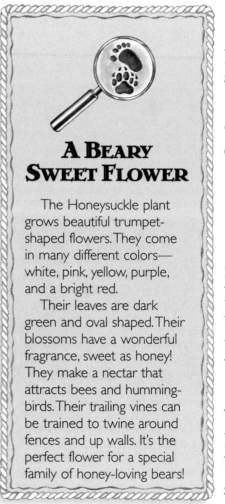

A BEARY SWEET FLOWER

The Honeysuckle plant grows beautiful trumpet-shaped flowers. They come in many different colors—white, pink, yellow, purple, and a bright red.

Their leaves are dark green and oval shaped. Their blossoms have a wonderful fragrance, sweet as honey! They make a nectar that attracts bees and humming-birds. Their trailing vines can be trained to twine around fences and up walls. It's the perfect flower for a special family of honey-loving bears!

High in the rugged Big Log Mountains, there's a secret place that no child has ever seen. The brambleberries are as sweet as candy. The trees are perfect for climbing.

And frisky bear cubs grow healthy and strong on homemade honey cakes. This special place is called . . . Honey Pine Woods.

THE BEARY FAMILY

The Beary family has lived in Honey Pine Woods for generations. And for generations the Bearys have had adventures their neighbors talk about even to this day. In fact, most every evening somewhere in the woods a cub begs for just one more Beary Tale before they go to bed.

These Beary Tales begin with Violet and Boone. They began their life together in a cozy log cabin that Boone built in the heart of the woods. It took Violet's breath away when he first showed it to her. Boone, a sentimental old bear, carved "A Home Sweet Home for My Violet" on a ceiling beam that day. Violet filled the cabin with music and love. Together they turned that cabin into a home.

For a wedding gift, Grandpa Buzz gave Violet and Boone a huge pot of his best berry blossom honey. Granny Rose gave them a rare red honeysuckle vine from her garden. Violet planted it by the front porch.

Granny Rose has a real green thumb with plants, but this prize vine amazed even Granny! It was enormous and covered with blossoms. In fact, it very nearly covered up the whole front of the cabin. Hardly a window or a door was visible!

When Boone saw it, he laughed so hard that his pants split and tears spilled out of his eyes. Violet didn't think it was funny until she stepped back to take a look. Then she started giggling, too! He kissed her dirt-smudged cheek and said, "If I didn't know better, I'd think I built this cottage of Honeysuckle."

Granny Rose eventually tamed the vine with her pruning sheers. But Boone began to call the cabin their cozy little "Honeysuckle Cottage." The name stuck.

THE BEARY CUBS

Dusty was the first cub to call Honeysuckle Cottage home. He was followed by a giggly cubette named Ashley and a chipper little cub they all called JJ.

Dusty was born early in the spring, just after the first thaw, when the air was still wintry crisp and pine scented. The first thing proud Papa Boone did was to carve Dusty's birth date onto one of the sturdy beams in the little attic nook that would eventually become Dusty's very own room. It was a tradition that would continue throughout Dusty's life. Onto those same wooden beams,

Papa carved a tiny cub's shoe to remember the day Dusty took his first step. When Dusty got an award for reading the most library books, Papa carved a book in honor of the occasion. And Dusty helped Papa carve a Bearball and bat to remember the day he hit his first home run.

It's one of Dusty's favorite traditions.

GREAT GRANDPA GRIZ ON THE HUNT

Dusty's Great Great Grandbears were one of the first pioneer families to come to the Big Log Mountains during the Golden Honey Rush. They left the comfort of the city to live in the wild woods. (Mama says that's where Dusty inherited his love for adventure.)

Dusty's Great Grandpa Griz had the first Beary adventure on Big Log Mountain. Young Griz enjoyed making the other cubs laugh, so one day he went hunting for firewood with a honey pot perched on his head. But the joke was on Griz. The honey pot slipped down and covered his eyes. He ran blindly stumbling through the woods until he tripped over a big hollow log filled with honey. When he looked around, he saw that the woods were rich with the tastiest honey any pioneer bear had ever known!

He ran back to camp, his grizzled fur all covered with the gooey treasure, a-hootin' and a-hollerin', "Honey in the Pine Woods! Honey in the Pine Woods!" The words bounced back and forth between the peaks of the Big Log Mountains and echoed back, "Honey Pine Woods! Honey Pine Woods!" Every bear liked the sound of it so much that they officially named the place Honey Pine Woods.

A SECRET HIDING PLACE

Great Grandpa Griz wasn't the only bear in Dusty's family to have an adventure while doing chores. Dusty's Granny Rose,

when she was a cubette, was given the job of digging up potatoes. She loved being in the garden, but she did not like digging up potatoes. It made her feel all grumbly inside.

But Little Rose absolutely loved to sing. So, her pa taught her a song. He told her that if she sang while she worked, the potatoes would be out in no time. She happily began to sing out loud and clear.

A BEARY FUNNY RIDDLE

Why did the farmer drive his steam roller over his potato field?

He was hungry for some mashed potatoes!

Ripe red apples, pumpkins round,
Leaves of crimson falling down,
Autumn blessings from the Lord
Thank Him now in one Accord.

Over and over she dug deep into the rich warm earth. Over and over she pulled out the hidden potatoes. And the autumn breeze danced around her and carried her words away in a delightful tumble of leaves.

But her singing stopped when, to her amazement, she discovered something buried in the dirt. It was a rusted metal box and inside it was the recipe

for a delicious treat. Honey Cakes! The most delicious honey cakes a bear could ever want. Long ago Granny had buried it there for safekeeping. That night the whole family dined on mashed potatoes and sweet, warm honey cakes.

Since that time, all cubs in Honey Pine Woods grow big and strong eating honey cakes made from Granny Rose's recipe.

MAMA'S PLAN

Dusty had grown up hearing Mama talk about Beary family adventures—adventures that happened even while doing something as ordinary as chores. But, he had always thought of them as just stories. Chores were *not* an adventure to him. In fact, he didn't like doing chores at all.

He was supposed to keep his room clean. He wished that he liked cleaning, but no matter how hard he tried, it always made him grumpy and cross. So, he avoided doing it. Mess piled upon mess until he didn't even want to go into his room. It was such a mess that he  often lost his homework under piles of clutter. And he could never find his Bearball cards when he wanted to trade one with his best friend Rusty, the cinnamon bear.

It was after one very grumpy day that Mama decided Dusty needed a little adventure in his life. She went to her pantry. There behind the brambleberry preserves was the chore jar that Granny Rose had passed on to her. She smiled as she pulled it out and dusted it off.

"We'll begin tomorrow," she whispered with anticipation.

It is here that these Beary Tales, Dusty's very own adventures, begin.

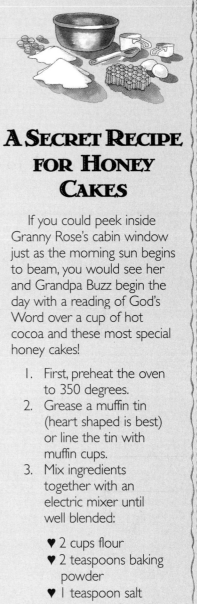

A SECRET RECIPE FOR HONEY CAKES

If you could peek inside Granny Rose's cabin window just as the morning sun begins to beam, you would see her and Grandpa Buzz begin the day with a reading of God's Word over a cup of hot cocoa and these most special honey cakes!

1. First, preheat the oven to 350 degrees.
2. Grease a muffin tin (heart shaped is best) or line the tin with muffin cups.
3. Mix ingredients together with an electric mixer until well blended:

   ♥ 2 cups flour
   ♥ 2 teaspoons baking powder
   ♥ 1 teaspoon salt
   ♥ 3/4 cup soft butter
   ♥ 1/4 cup honey
   ♥ 3/4 cup milk
   ♥ 1 teaspoon vanilla
   ♥ 3 eggs

Pour batter into muffin tin and bake for 20 minutes or until golden honey brown. You can eat these plain, sprinkled with powdered sugar, or with frosting.

"Work happily together" (*Romans 12:16 TLB*).

DUSTY'S LOST TREASURE

KEY THOUGHT

Teamwork is the key to making any job easier. Add a little creativity and it may even become an adventure!

The sweet smell of homemade honey cakes drifted up the well-worn stairs of Honeysuckle Cottage and into the cozy attic nook that Dusty called his own. He breathed a sleepy-eyed morning yawn. Downstairs he heard the joyful clatter of pots and pans. Mama was busy in the kitchen. Her cheery voice sang:

Ripe red apples, pumpkins round,
leaves of crimson falling down . . .

Dusty pulled his warm covers up close under his chin and began to think about his plans for the day. Rusty, the cinnamon bear, was Dusty's best friend. They both loved hiking, playing Bearball, and planning adventures.

One day, while hiking on the windy trail below the Great Bear Cliffs, they had spied an old cave. Their imaginations ran wild, dreaming of the treasures they might find there.

"Maybe we'll find a treasure map left by an old grizzly pirate!" guessed Dusty. "Or a map that'll lead us to Lost Golden Honey Hive!" he added mysteriously.

Just the idea of finding treasure was enough to get the cubs excited. They immediately planned a grand exploration of the cave.

It took them two days to gather the equipment for their trip. When they confided their plan to Grandpa Buzz, he offered to let them use his lanterns and canteens. Rusty donated a broken shovel and a bit of rope he had found while looking around at the dump. And Dusty packed some leftover sweets he'd saved from his birthday.

Now everything lay secretly stashed behind the granite boulders that lined the entrance to the trail. Today after school, they would conquer the cave together.

MORNING MADNESS!

Looking at the cuckoo clock on the wall, Dusty realized that he had been daydreaming in his bed far too long. "Yikes! Mr. Bookman will have my hide if I'm late to school." He bolted out of bed and began to frantically search for his overalls. It was no easy task because the floor of his room was littered from one end to the other with heaps and mounds of junk.

In his rush, Dusty stumbled over his Bearball bat and twisted his ankle. "Yee-Oowch!" he growled as he held his ankle and jumped up and down. He finally landed on the floor with a firm thud! It made such an earth-shattering noise that, moments later, Mama and Papa breathlessly appeared at his door.

"Dusty, are you all right?" Mama asked, still dusted from head to toe with cinnamon sugar from the morning baking.

"I'm NOT all right! JJ left his toy down there, and I tripped on it. He's always leaving his stuff in my room," he said pointing to one tiny action hero which lay innocently atop the mass of clutter that was clearly Dusty's own stuff.

Papa just stood there in his nightshirt, gazing at the room in disbelief. He had

never seen such a sight! Dusty's things were scattered from one end of the room to the other. "Son, did a tornado strike your room?"

Dusty lowered his head and, with a sheepish grin on his face, replied, "I'll clean it up when I get home from school, Papa." Right away he realized what he had said. He couldn't clean his room today. He had to meet Rusty after school. He wanted to take it all back, but the stern look on Papa's face stopped him.

"Stupid chores!" he muttered as he kicked at a pile of clothes. "How am I gonna explain this to Rusty?"

The kitchen timer began buzzing. Before Mama turned to go back downstairs she reminded him, "The bus will be here in a few minutes, so you'd better hurry! And don't forget to take your umbrella; storm clouds are rolling in."

BEAT THE CLOCK

Hey, kids! Did you know you can make chore time fun with a kitchen timer? That's right! Just set the timer to 10 or 15 minutes, then blast off to clean your room before the bell on the timer dings!

Dusty's search turned frantic as he dug through the rumpled clothes on the floor. He could only find the overalls with the berry stains on the knees. They would just have to do. He bumped his head searching for his homework under the desk. He found it. But he also discovered that a glass of water had spilled on it so the words were all blurry and hard to read. "Oh, brother!" he exclaimed. He stuffed the soggy wad into his backpack anyway.

With the last few minutes he had, Dusty brushed his fur, but he had no time to find his umbrella or eat breakfast. With a heavy heart and a growling stomach, he raced out the door to catch the school bus.

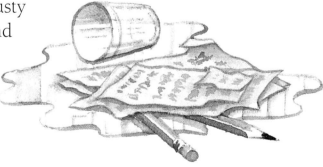

WHAT A DAY!

As the bus made its herky-jerky start toward Meadowbrook School for Bears, Dusty realized that he had left his lunch at home. He searched his backpack for something to eat, but he only found a half-eaten honey bar

13

covered with backpack fuzz.

"You'll be a hungry cub today!" Dusty grumbled.

What a day Dusty had! All morning Rusty gave him dirty looks from across the room. Mr. Bookman made him stay in during recess to recopy his soggy homework. At lunch time, he watched everyone enjoying honey cakes while he ate his stale honey bar. When the bell for the second recess sounded, Dusty ran for the door. He was hoping for a good game of catch. But Mama was right, a storm had blown in. It was raining fast and hard.

The rain didn't let up for the rest of the day. By the time the school bus dropped him off, everything in Honey Pine Woods was soaked through and through.

Dusty dragged himself over Moss Covered Bridge and up Crooked Path to Honeysuckle Cottage. He walked into the cabin, a tired and soggy cub. And he was hungry enough to "eat the bark off a tree" as Granny Rose would say.

ASHLEY'S RIDDLE

What is a bear cub called after he is nine months old?

10 months old!

SURPRISE!

At first, he thought no one was home. He changed his mind, though, when he saw a tiny beam of light coming from behind the door and heard a giggle.

That Ashley! thought Dusty. *She's such a giggly cubette.*

"Ashley, I know you're back there. Come out from behind that door," demanded Dusty, who was in no mood for a game of hide-and-seek.

"Okay, but close your eyes first," replied the giggle. Dusty impatiently closed his eyes.

Three excited voices yelled, "SURPRISE!"

The last voice was that of JJ who squeaked with

gley, "*Thurprithe, Duthty!*" (His S's always sounded a little more like Th's.)

When Dusty opened his eyes he truly was surprised. Standing there, peeking out from behind the door, was Mama wearing a safari hat and a big grin! Ashley stood there giggling as she peeked out from under the bucket that she had placed on her head. Little JJ was down on the floor with a honey pot on his head. In one paw he held a flashlight, and in the other, he dragged his floppy Teddy Jingles by one arm.

Dusty was so surprised that his eyes looked almost as big as two apples from Granny Rose's orchard. At once, everyone was laughing. Everyone, including Dusty!

"What are you bears doing?" Dusty finally asked once things quieted down.

Mama replied with the most serious face she could muster, "Why, we're going on a treasure hunt with you, of course!" She removed her safari hat and placed it on Dusty's rain-soaked head. "But first, we must get you some dry clothes and some of my cinnamon bear cookies."

THE ADVENTURE BEGINS

After they finished their snack, Mama brought out the jar that Granny Rose had given her. Through the wavy glass they could see folded cards. "The adventure you will have today came from this very jar." She opened the lid and pulled out a card marked "Going on a Treasure Hunt!"

Then she handed Dusty a scroll. When he unrolled it, he saw "Dusty's Lost Treasure Map" written in crayon across the top and a drawing of Dusty's attic room. Beside the drawing, was a list of all the items that Dusty had lost lately.

"You are the great Indiana Jones in search of lost treasures. We are your

MAMA'S CINNAMON BEAR COOKIES

- ♥ 3/4 cup butter or margarine
- ♥ 1 1/4 cup sugar
- ♥ 1 egg
- ♥ 2 teaspoons vanilla
- ♥ 2 1/2 cup flour
- ♥ 1/2 teaspoon salt
- ♥ cinnamon and sugar mixture
- ♥ Raisins or chocolate chips for eyes

Beat first 4 ingredients at high speed until fluffy. Mix in flour and salt until a stiff dough forms. Wrap dough in plastic and chill for 2 hours. (This is a good time to tidy up the kitchen.)

Divide dough into 8 equal pieces. Out of each piece form 3 balls, 1 large and 2 small. Place larger ball on cookie sheet for the face and attach the 2 smaller balls above it for ears. Flatten slightly and sprinkle with a mixture of cinnamon and sugar. Press in 2 raisins or chocolate chips for eyes. Bake at 350° on a greased cookie sheet for 8 minutes.

search and rescue team. Together, we are going to find your treasures and restore them to their rightful place in your room."

"Sounds like cleaning my room, Mama," said Dusty with one eyebrow raised.

"Nonsense!" Mama declared. "You'll never have an adventure if you look at things that way. Ordinary bears see chores as just one of the bare necessities of life. But you come from a long line of *extra*ordinary bears. We look at all sorts of ordinary things as opportunities for adventure!"

"Even chores?" Dusty questioned.

"Especially chores!" Mama assured. "Why, if it weren't for your Great Grandpa Griz doing his chores, Honey Pine Woods might never have been discovered!"

"Really?" the cubs marveled.

"Oh, yes!"

Then she stood and announced, "Let the adventure begin!"

"But, Mama need*th* a hat, too!" noticed JJ.

"I'll find one!" said Ashley. In moments, she was back with one of Grandpa Buzz's old beekeeper hats complete with netting. Mama peeked out from behind the netting and gave the thumbs-up sign. Now she was ready, too.

Dusty pointed toward the stairs, and said, "We shall begin in the closet!"

He bravely led them past the cushy sofa, up the well-worn stairs, and into Dusty's own attic room. In the closet, things were examined one by one. When something on the list was found they would check it off and announce, "The treasure has been found!" Then they would return the item to its proper place.

Once the closet was done, Dusty led them on

a dangerous search through the toy box. They even got up enough courage to search under the bed! They found things in the most unusual places. Dusty's umbrella was behind some clothes on his bookshelf. His favorite Bearball card was in the pocket of his raincoat. They found the raincoat stuffed in the bottom of his sweater drawer. In all, twenty-two-and-a-half lost treasures were found. (The "half" treasure was one Bearball shoe. Dusty had given Rusty the other shoe to carry home some berries they had found.) But the best treasure was the very last thing they found.

They stood back to admire the change in Dusty's room. Then Ashley exclaimed, "I saw something sparkle over there! Right there where JJ was just shining the flashlight!" She pointed to the far corner of the room to a spot just below the cuckoo clock. JJ eagerly shone his flashlight on the spot. Sure enough, through a crack in the wall, they could see something sparkle.

"It's a secret hiding place!" whispered Dusty in amazement. "How come I never noticed it before?" They all turned and gave him a look. He just grinned and said, "Oh yeah! Kinda messy before, huh?"

"Well, open it up!" Ashley exclaimed, jumping until her curly fur practically bounced.

The cubs tried pushing and pulling, poking and banging. Finally JJ stomped his foot and said, "Why won't that *thilly* thing open?" With that little stomp, the hidden door opened, and the source of the sparkle was clearly seen by all.

"It's a gold pocket watch!" Dusty declared. He fingered the golden chain

and wiped the dust from the watch cover and saw a delicate engraving of Honey Pine Woods.

He carefully wound the watch. It immediately began *"tick-tick-ticking."* Then, he opened it and gasped. Tiny golden bear figures began to move about. They bobbed up and down or seesawed to the regular motion of the gears. The tiniest *"ding"* announced each new hour. It was the most unusual watch Dusty had ever seen.

"I *thee thomething elthe!*" whispered JJ. "I*th's a note!*"

As everyone peered over his shoulder, Dusty began to read.

GOD'S WORD IS BEARY GOOD

God has a special plan for every single person! Papa shared with Dusty a scripture verse that he had learned as a young cub.

"I know the plans I have for you," declares the Lord, "plans to prosper you and not to harm you, plans to give you hope and a future" (Jeremiah 29:11).

To Our Son Dusty,

As you grow up, you have times when you wonder about things. But there is something you never need to wonder about . . . Your Heavenly Father loves you and we do, too. No matter what! Knowing that makes discovering God's plan for your life easier. We can't tell you exactly what God's plan is, but one thing we know for sure; it will be an adventure!

Your Great Grandpa Griz bought this pocket watch with the money from his first honey harvest. He had a wonderful adventure discovering that honey. We're passing it on to you with this prayer. "Lord Jesus, Bless our Dusty. Help him to honor You all the days of his life and reward him with a life that's rich with adventure!"

"Love, your very own Mama and Papa," finished Papa in a crackly voice.

Dusty ran to Mama and Papa and hugged them till they could hardly breathe. "Oh, thank you, Papa. Thank you, Mama! That was incredible! I never thought I'd find a treasure in my very own room!"

THE AMAZING BEARY CUBS

The cubs made a terrific team! In the days that followed, they each took turns leading search and rescue expeditions all through the cottage. Each time they found something, they wrote it down on a strip of colored paper. Then the strip was added to the paper chain that hung across the rafters in the living room. The word spread throughout the woods and soon they were helping everyone find all sorts of lost things. Soon the chain stretched all the way around the room! Next, they volunteered to help Rusty find a few things he had misplaced.

And everyone began calling them "The Amazing Beary Cubs."

From that time on, things were different around the Beary house. Though Dusty's room still got messy sometimes, he really didn't mind cleaning it. When Ashley or JJ needed help with something, Dusty would remember how willing they had been to help him, and he would offer to give them a hand. And whenever he wound up the golden pocket watch, he would wonder what wonderful adventures God had in store for him.

PAPER CHAIN FUN!

Start your own paper chain to measure your accomplishments. Begin by cutting several strips of colorful paper, all the same length. For every goal you complete, whether it's a book you've read or a chore you've finished, you can add to your chain by pasting them together, link by link. You'll have lots of fun watching your chain grow!

LET'S TALK ABOUT BEARY TALES

▶ How do you think Dusty felt when his Mama and Papa saw how messy his room was?

▶ What did Mama do to make cleaning Dusty's room seem more like a fun adventure?

▶ Teamwork is when others pitch in to help. Share some reasons why you think Dusty was glad Ashley, JJ, and Mama helped him.

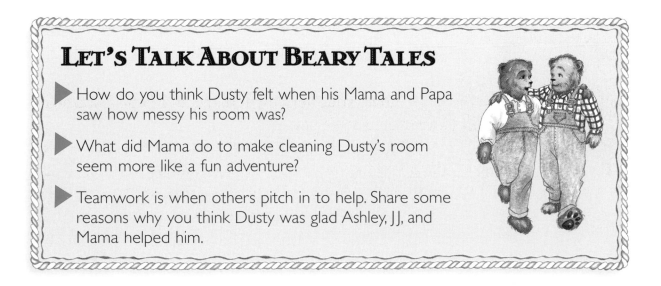

"In the same way, let your light shine before men,
that they may see your good deeds and praise
your Father in heaven" (*Matthew 5:16*).

KEY THOUGHT
The best good deeds are done just for love.
Sometimes they're the only thing that will open a stubborn heart.

lang-Clang rang out the old copper bell atop Meadowbrook School
for Bears. It was the start of every cubs' favorite season—summer
vacation! Cubs swarmed out of the little red schoolhouse like bees
in search of honey.

"Hurry up, slow poke!" Rusty the cinnamon bear shouted as he sprinted
up the cobblestone steps of Crooked Path.

"I'll get there before you do!" huffed Dusty, following close behind.

The race was on! They headed for a homemade fort hidden in the pines
behind Honeysuckle Cottage. The winner would be declared "Chief Bear in
Charge" for the summer!

The last two years Rusty had won the race by a nose. This year Dusty was
determined to win. He had been secretly training. He had hiked the trails of
Great Bear Cliffs to build up his strength. He had also drawn a map to find the
shortest route from school to The Fort. They had always raced up Crooked

Path to get to The Fort. Now he could see that it was shorter to cut through Mr. McGruder's place, but the thought of it made him nervous.

Mr. McGruder was a gruff old bear. All the other cubs called him Old Grizzle Face because he snarled like a mean old grizzly bear when he got mad. And it seemed as if he was always mad. But Dusty wanted to win so badly he wouldn't allow even mean old Mr. McGruder to stop him.

THE BEAR FACTS

The Grizzly is a bear found in western North America and is considered an endangered species in many places. They are named for their furry brown coat sprinkled with white hairs, which gives them the appearance of being "grizzled" or streaked with gray.

THE GREAT RACE

Rusty was nearly fifty strides ahead when Dusty made his move. He ran straight toward Mr. McGruder's place. When he was sure he was safely in the lead, he looked back. He wanted to see how far behind Rusty was. Instead, what he saw running straight toward him was the looming figure of a grizzled old bear waving a big stick high in the air.

"M c G r u d e r!" Dusty shouted fearfully. He began to run hard and fast. Every time he risked a look, there would be Mr. McGruder, shortening the distance between them.

Then it happened. *Thunk!* Dusty ran head first into a huge beehive that dangled from a tree branch. It was an instant honey bath. His fur was coated from head to toe with the sticky, gooey stuff. A moment later, angry bees exploded out of what was left of the smashed hive and attacked Dusty's head. He couldn't decide which was worse—the bees or McGruder!

There was no time to think. He just ran waving his arms and shrieking all the way to Strawberry Creek. There he dove into the stream, leaving only his furry nose peeking out.

In a little while, Dusty heard sounds from the shore. He came out of the water to see Rusty rolling on the ground, laughing and holding his belly.

"You should have seen yourself, Dusty! McGruder . . . bees. . . !" he sputtered.

Dusty plopped down on the warm, dry sand and began to pick the leaves and dirt out of his sticky fur. "Very funny. Very funny, Rusty."

"I'm sorry. But it really was a funny sight to see." Rusty tried hard not to laugh.

"I bet it wouldn't be so funny if it were *you*," Dusty frowned.

"I tell you what! After what I just saw, I'd say you earned the title this year. Congratulations, you're Chief Bear in Charge!" declared Rusty.

Dusty didn't feel like a winner.

THE FORT

The Fort was built in a twisted old tree. Dusty and Papa had worked on it for a whole week. Mama had sewn curtains for the windows. Ashley and JJ had dipped their paws in colorful paint and stamped them on the pine-scented walls. Grandpa Buzz brought over butter-colored hay to carpet the floor. It was a perfect place for sleepovers. And, that's just where the cubs planned to spend their first night of vacation.

Dusty, Ashley, JJ, and Rusty were stretched out on the floor, gazing up at the night sky. Dusty sighed into the quietness, "This is the life."

"Yep! Thi*th* i*th* the life!" squeaked JJ as he rolled over on top of his partially finished honey cake. He sat up, peeled the treat from his little belly, and ate it!

"That's sick, JJ!" Ashley groaned.

JJ squeaked, "Tha*th*'s not *th*ick. It'*th* honey cake!"

"Speaking of honey," Rusty kidded, "did you know that Dusty had a honey bath today?"

Rusty told the cubs about Mr. McGruder and the

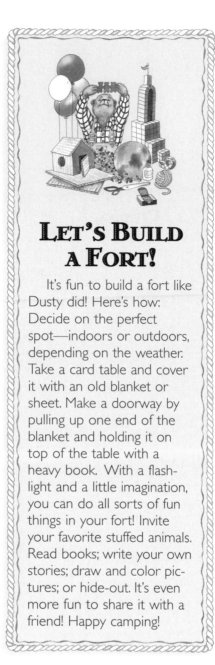

LET'S BUILD A FORT!

It's fun to build a fort like Dusty did! Here's how: Decide on the perfect spot—indoors or outdoors, depending on the weather. Take a card table and cover it with an old blanket or sheet. Make a doorway by pulling up one end of the blanket and holding it on top of the table with a heavy book. With a flashlight and a little imagination, you can do all sorts of fun things in your fort! Invite your favorite stuffed animals. Read books; write your own stories; draw and color pictures; or hide-out. It's even more fun to share it with a friend! Happy camping!

swarm of bees. The cubs laughed till their sides hurt!

Ashley stood to speak. "There is something—*mysterious*—about Mr. McGruder," she confided in a hushed tone of voice.

"Let me ask you this," she said as she paced slowly back and forth. "When a delivery cart ran over that squirrel last week . . . who was seen sneaking off with the body?…McGruder!" she declared as she turned on her heels.

"Who has, in fact, been around when other poor animals have disappeared?…McGruder!" she went on.

"If that is his *real* name," she finished with a glint in her eye.

For a moment they all just stared at her.

"You know what I think?" asked Rusty, who was not to be outdone by Ashley. "I think Old Grizzle Face McGruder . . . eats woodland creatures!"

"Stop it! You're scaring JJ," warned Dusty. He gave JJ a reassuring hug.

Rusty leaned closer and whispered, "Okay. But just think about this. What will you do if you walk up Crooked Path some night and find yourself face to face with the horrible Grizzle Face himself?"

"Aw, just go to sleep, Rusty. I think we've all had enough stories for tonight."

That night Dusty's dreams were filled with angry bees and bear cub stew and Old Grizzle Face McGruder.

BACK AT HOME

In the morning the Bearys planned to head off for a day of family fun . . . after their chores. They closed their eyes before selecting a card from Granny

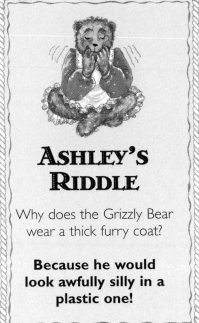

Rose's jar. Papa would wash the dishes. Mama would sweep the porch. Ashley would put the toys and games away. JJ would take the trash out. Dusty was the last to choose.

He read his card out loud. The title read "Love Bears All Things" and under it was printed, "Do something kind for someone."

He began to think about helping Rusty fix his bike. Dusty thought he knew how to fix it. . .

ASHLEY'S RIDDLE

Why does the Grizzly Bear wear a thick furry coat?

Because he would look awfully silly in a plastic one!

Mama interrupted his thoughts, though. "Let's do this one as a family," she suggested. "Who do we know that could use some tender loving care?"

"Granny Rose and Grandpa Buzz!" said Ashley.

"Rusty!" added Dusty.

"Teddy Jingle*th!*" JJ chimed in, holding up his favorite floppy teddy.

"How about someone who doesn't have many friends?" asked Mama.

"Old Grizzle Face doesn't have many friends," whispered Ashley to Dusty privately.

Unfortunately, Papa heard the comment. "There will be no name-calling in this cottage!"

Dusty pleaded, "But Papa . . ." Dusty told Papa everything that had happened with Mr. McGruder.

"I'll agree that Mr. McGruder is a gruff old bear, but that's no reason to call any bear a name. How do you cubs like it when someone calls you a bad name?" asked Papa.

Mama added, "Sometimes bears who are gruff and grouchy outside are really sad and lonely inside. Bears like that need someone to be kind to them."

"I suggest we make Mr. McGruder our family project," said Papa.

The cubs weren't so sure.

"He'll probably *eat* us!" said Ashley, her eyes big and wide.

"JJ *th*tay home," said JJ as he hugged Teddy Jingles.

"Nonsense!" Mama said. "We have been adventurous bears for

generations! We can't be put off by a grouchy old bear. But, I'll admit, Mr. McGruder will be a challenge." Mama rubbed her chin with her paw as she thought. "Now, what should we do?"

Ashley had a great idea. "Mr. McGruder sure could use some sweetening up. How about giving him some of our best berry-blossom honey?"

They all giggled and agreed that a dose of honey was just what he needed.

"Okay! How should we give it to him?" asked Mama.

"Don't look at me!" replied Dusty.

Mama finally decided. "We'll do it secretly. It won't be easy, but it will be an adventure!"

SECRET ACTS OF KINDNESS

A jar of their best berry-blossom honey was wrapped in a colorful sheet of paper that JJ had decorated. Papa attached a note that he nicknamed his "Handwritten Bear Hug." It read:

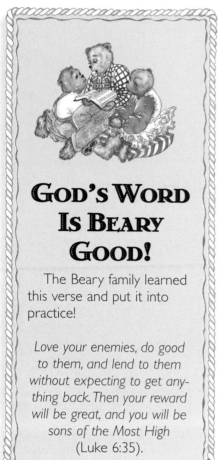

God's Word Is Beary Good!

The Beary family learned this verse and put it into practice!

Love your enemies, do good to them, and lend to them without expecting to get anything back. Then your reward will be great, and you will be sons of the Most High (Luke 6:35).

A Beary Special Gift Just for You

As planned, Mama, Ashley, and JJ watched from the safety of the overgrown gooseberry bushes while Dusty and Papa crept up the path to Mr. McGruder's cabin.

They were almost there when a pinecone fell out of a tree and smashed onto the roof of the cabin. Dusty's heart pounded hard. They stood perfectly still, listening to the sounds that came from inside the cabin. Papa placed his finger to his lips to keep Dusty quiet. But Papa didn't have to worry, Dusty was so scared he *couldn't* talk!

Once the coast was clear, they placed their gift on the front porch and then joined the others. They had almost given up waiting when the cabin door opened. Mr. McGruder stood there with his paws stretched out. He let out a huge yawn. Mr McGruder had a ferocious-looking set of teeth!

When he discovered the gift, he held it at a distance as he turned it in his paws. Then he read the note with the most puzzled look on his face. He removed the paper and saw the honey. Once again his teeth showed, but he wasn't growling this time—he was grinning! It was probably the first grin that any bear had ever seen on Mr. McGruder's face.

He turned and took the gift into his cabin, and they all looked at each other in disbelief. Was there really more than growls and scowls to Mr. McGruder?

Over the next few weeks they did other secret kind deeds for Mr. McGruder. Papa and JJ returned several times to leave little gifts. Mama and Ashley brought tasty home-baked goodies. They would hide them in the silliest places. One morning Mr. McGruder found their mouth-watering cornbread 'n' honey muffins tucked into his water bucket!

Dusty enjoyed the challenge of finding new things to do without being seen. One day Mr. McGruder found a fresh pile of kindling wood stacked

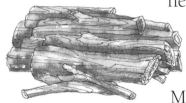

neatly beside his kitchen door. Another day he went to the garden and found that it had been watered. In time, their kindness began to change Mr. McGruder, too. His heart softened.

A SECRET DISCOVERED

Dusty arrived bright and early one morning to put the finishing touches on some raking when Mr. McGruder snuck up behind him. Suddenly, Dusty felt the heavy weight of a paw on his shoulder.

"What do you think you're doing?" asked Mr. McGruder in his gruff old voice.

Dusty stammered, "I, I . . . You see, I was

FINGERPRINT FUN!

You can make your own "Handwritten Bear Hug" for someone you care about. You'll need:

- ♥ Paper or 3x5 index cards
- ♥ Stamp pad (brown ink is good)
- ♥ Colored markers

Press one finger on the stamp pad, then onto the paper to create your fingerprint. Make 2 or 3 more fingerprints. Then with a black marker draw teddy bear faces on the prints. Add ears, a nose and a smile for a beary happy greeting! Print the words "A handwritten bear hug just for you!"

You can decorate the card even more by drawing balloons, flowers, stars, or a rainbow! Send it to someone who could use some cheering up.

ASHLEY'S CORNBREAD 'N' HONEY MUFFINS

- ♥ 1 cup sifted all-purpose flour
- ♥ 3/4 cup yellow cornmeal
- ♥ 4 teaspoons baking powder
- ♥ 4 tablespoons sugar
- ♥ 1/2 teaspoon salt
- ♥ 1 large egg
- ♥ 1 cup milk
- ♥ 3 tablespoons melted butter
- ♥ 1 cup thawed frozen corn (optional)

To begin, preheat the oven to 400°. Place liners in your muffin tin or generously grease each cup. In a large bowl, sift flour with cornmeal, baking powder, and salt. In a separate bowl mix together the egg, milk, and melted butter. Pour the liquid mixture into the dry ingredients and blend gently, do not beat. Stir in the corn until well blended.

Fill lined muffin cups 3/4 full. Bake 20 minutes or until muffins are golden brown and firm to the touch. Serve piping hot with enough butter and honey to drizzle on top. (Mama says honey is not a safe treat for children under 2 years. In this recipe another substitute such as jam may be used.)

raking, sir." Then he gulped and took a step back.

"You're not going anywhere. Tell me *why* you're doing these things?" Mr. McGruder insisted.

"I don't know why, sir. I guess we just wanted to see you smile," offered Dusty meekly.

"What do you mean? '*We*'?" His voice was softer now.

"My family and me. We just wanted to see you smile."

When Dusty realized that he had just given their secret away, he was so disappointed that he dropped his rake. As it happened, it fell right on top of his foot. One of the sharp tines dug in deep, and Dusty began to bleed. He looked up at Mr. McGruder with tears in his eyes.

But Dusty could hardly believe what he saw! Mr. McGruder was smiling and looking down at him with tears in *his* eyes. In a moment, Dusty could see that Mr. McGruder's angry scowl was gone. He was all softness and fur.

"Oh my dear cub, I must see to that cut," Mr. McGruder said as he took Dusty into his cabin.

What Dusty saw in the cabin was just as amazing as the change in Mr. McGruder. One whole wall from the floor to the ceiling was filled with cages. In the cages were little animals that looked sick or injured. On the other wall were stacks of doctors' books.

Mr. McGruder didn't *eat* helpless animals, he tried to *cure* them!

Mr. McGruder bandaged Dusty's injury as lovingly as he cared for the creatures that shared his cabin.

"Would you like a glass of lemonade?" Mr. McGruder asked when he was finished. Somehow, it just seemed right to say "Yes."

Dusty learned that Mr. McGruder had once chased his friends to keep them from throwing rocks. The tree the cubs had been aiming for held a nest of newborn songbirds. The squirrel Mr. McGruder had carried off was now recovering in a softly padded cage. And the day he had chased after Dusty? Well, he had just been trying to keep him from running into that huge hanging beehive.

An Unexpected Friendship

Mr. McGruder and Dusty spent a lot of time together that summer. Mr. McGruder taught Dusty how to take care of the animals. Dusty taught Mr. McGruder about being a friend. Dusty nicknamed him "Doc." Doc nicknamed Dusty "Wa-han-to." (It means "good friend" in the ancient language of Indian bear tribes.)

Eventually the warm glow of summer began to fade. As the bus made its way back to Meadowbrook School for Bears, Dusty realized that he had learned a lot that summer. He found out that he actually liked doing secret good deeds. And, through it all, he had gained a true friend in Doc. Mama was right. It had been an adventure.

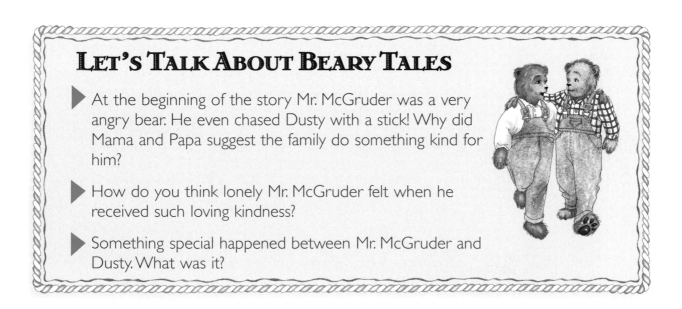

Let's Talk About Beary Tales

▶ At the beginning of the story Mr. McGruder was a very angry bear. He even chased Dusty with a stick! Why did Mama and Papa suggest the family do something kind for him?

▶ How do you think lonely Mr. McGruder felt when he received such loving kindness?

▶ Something special happened between Mr. McGruder and Dusty. What was it?

"Keep your lives free from the love of money and be content with what you have, because God has said, 'Never will I leave you; never will I forsake you.'" (*Hebrews 13:5*).

A SURPRISE FOR DUSTY'S EYES

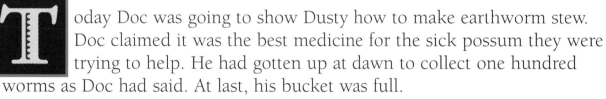

KEY THOUGHT

The key to contentment is realizing that the gift of love is the greatest treasure of all.

Today Doc was going to show Dusty how to make earthworm stew. Doc claimed it was the best medicine for the sick possum they were trying to help. He had gotten up at dawn to collect one hundred worms as Doc had said. At last, his bucket was full.

Dusty whistled a happy tune as he walked toward Doc's cabin. But his mind was on making stew, not on the noise brewing overhead. That's why the squirrel's ambush took him by surprise. Dusty's head was the target, and the squirrel hit the mark. In a flash, the squirrel disappeared down Dusty's shirt. He tickled Dusty until he collapsed into a giggling heap covered with squirming worms.

It was hard to believe that this was the same squirrel who had been run over by a delivery cart. Doc and Dusty had spent hours feeding and caring for the frail creature. When he finally got well, they named him "Lucky" because they figured he had been really lucky to survive the accident.

Dusty and Lucky became great friends. When the day arrived that Lucky was ready to return to the woods, Dusty was sad to see him go. He tearfully waved good-bye from the front porch as Lucky scampered off. But when Dusty

came home from school, there sat Lucky staring at him through the attic window, wearing a wide squirrelly grin!

A HIDDEN SECRET

Dusty gathered the worms back into the bucket, and said, "Come on, Lucky! Let's go find Doc!" They raced into the cabin. There, sitting on the mantle, was a note from Doc.

Dusty, No lesson today! There's a sick raccoon stuck under Mrs. Nuthatch's back porch. Please feed the animals before you leave. Thanks, Wa-han-to.

Your Friend, Doc

While Dusty fed the patients, Lucky helped out in his own way. He climbed to the very top of the bookshelf, fluffed up his bushy tail and began to dust. Suddenly, one hard swish sent a book tumbling from its place on the shelf. It fell with a huge *slap* onto the wood floor below.

"What's this?" Dusty mumbled to himself as he reached down to pick it up. It was an old medical book. There were the usual medicines like homemade Swamp Mud Creme to treat insect bites. But one page caught his eye. It read,

Swirling clouds of dusty brown, Blowing winds that howl,
From the clearing in the pines, Look for the grizzly's jowl,
Risky journey wet and wild, Top of hill and count to five,
Shining there—a future bright, Lost Golden Honey Hive!

"LOST . . . GOLDEN . . . HONEY . . . HIVE?" Dusty read it over and over again, but he still couldn't believe his eyes. Every cub in Honey Pine Woods knew that old Indian legend!

THE LEGEND OF
LOST GOLDEN HONEY HIVE

The tribe was hungry and food was getting hard to find. Every brave had been sent on a hunt, when the elders heard the drum beat. The message? A great buffalo had been sighted. Their only hope was to send the young boy Straight Arrow.

Well, to make a long legend short, he got lost on the hunt. Straight Arrow's horse Lightning got spooked and ran away with everything, including his bow and arrow. His hope was all but gone, when he spotted a massive beehive in the trunk of a twisted old oak tree. There golden honey, a treasure more precious than gold, glistened in the sunlight.

Straight Arrow wanted to bring the whole hive back. Unfortunately, the only thing he had to carry it in was a small medicine bag that hung around his neck. But that little bag of honey turned out to be much more valuable than the buffalo. The buffalo would feed the tribe for a month, but that golden honey bought everything they needed for the whole year!

A SECRET IS REVEALED

A silly grin emerged on Dusty's face as he mouthed the word, "Treasure!"

Grabbing the book, he almost flew out of the cabin. Lucky eagerly followed along.

On the way home, all that Dusty could think of was the treasure! When the wind began to howl so loudly that it drowned out Lucky's chattering, Dusty didn't notice.

The sky turned brown as the wind stirred up huge clouds of dust. By the time Dusty reached home, he could hardly walk straight as blasts of gritty wind pushed against him. He lowered his head, clutched the book tightly to his chest, and hurled himself up the last two steps.

Everyone else had been inside Honeysuckle Cottage when The Great Wind had begun. They were all gathered in the living room to wait out the storm when Dusty burst through the door.

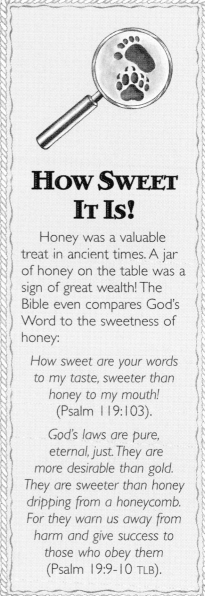

HOW SWEET IT IS!

Honey was a valuable treat in ancient times. A jar of honey on the table was a sign of great wealth! The Bible even compares God's Word to the sweetness of honey:

How sweet are your words to my taste, sweeter than honey to my mouth! (Psalm 119:103).

God's laws are pure, eternal, just. They are more desirable than gold. They are sweeter than honey dripping from a honeycomb. For they warn us away from harm and give success to those who obey them (Psalm 19:9-10 TLB).

"*Hah-huh, hah-huh,*" he breathed heavily as he leaned against the door.

"I'm so glad you're home safe!" Mama exclaimed with relief.

Dusty staggered to the couch and plopped down next to her. Then he held the book out for everyone to see.

"I'VE FOUND THE TREASURE!" he declared.

"It'*th* ju*tht* an old book!" chirped JJ.

"Let me see," Mama said.

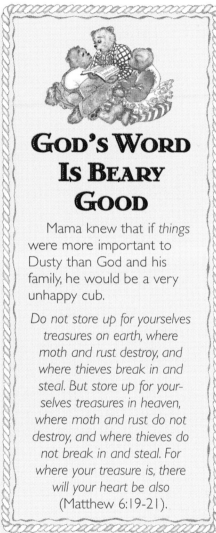

GOD'S WORD IS BEARY GOOD

Mama knew that if *things* were more important to Dusty than God and his family, he would be a very unhappy cub.

Do not store up for yourselves treasures on earth, where moth and rust destroy, and where thieves break in and steal. But store up for yourselves treasures in heaven, where moth and rust do not destroy, and where thieves do not break in and steal. For where your treasure is, there will your heart be also (Matthew 6:19-21).

"This poem is going to lead us to the treasure of Lost Golden Honey Hive!" Dusty explained. "We'll be rich!" Then he began to rattle off his long wish list: "I want a new fishing rod, a custom cherry red go-cart, a super deluxe Backwoods backpack, all of the Bearball cards in Cub World Toy Store . . ." Then he realized that everyone was staring at him. He blushed and added, "Oh! Ah . . . *and* we'll get lots of stuff for you, too."

Mama looked at Papa and they both slowly shook their heads.

"Looks like The Fever to me!" said Mama.

"Just what I was thinking, dear. A bad case of Golden Honey Fever," Papa declared.

"Du*thty'th* got a fever?" JJ worried.

"Not that kind of fever, JJ. It's Golden Honey Fever," Mama explained in a sad voice. "It struck some bears during the Golden Honey Rush. They didn't care a bit about anything or anybear, only their treasure. Your Granny Rose always said that The Fever was just a 'fancy name for old-fashioned greed.' But no matter how you say it, getting carried away with treasure hunting just leads to no good!"

"That's true!" agreed Papa as he turned to Dusty. "I seem to remember that you and Rusty went hunting for that very same treasure in an old cave. Have you forgotten what happened?"

Dusty lowered his head. He remembered it *very* well!

Papa put his thumbs in his overall straps and paused to think. "Let me see. As I remember you nearly fell off the cliffs when bats chased you out of that cave."

"But, Papa, it will be different this time—I have the poem," Dusty argued.

They talked and talked, but Dusty could not be talked out of his treasure-hunting dreams.

THE SEARCH FOR CLUES

The clock read 6:00 A.M., but it was still as dark as midnight in the house. Mama and Papa opened the front door and looked outside. Scattered over the yard were all sorts of blown-down and broken things from the wind the night before. When they walked outside to look at the cottage, they saw what had made it so dark inside. The wind had blown a thick coating of dust and mud on the windows!

"Well, it looks like a little cleanup is definitely in order this morning!" Papa said as he traced "Wash Me" with his finger in the dust. "How about if Mama and I work on the yard and you cubs try your paws at these windows?"

The cubs began soaping up the windows. Lucky even helped. Ashley and JJ laughed and drew pictures in the dust before washing them away with their sponges. Lucky dipped his tail in the suds, but he mostly splashed Ashley and JJ when they weren't looking. Dusty kept thinking about that poem.

"'Swirling clouds of dusty brown, Blowing winds that howl . . .'" he repeated to himself as he scrubbed away the dirt. It was then that an idea came to him. "Wait a minute! That could be The Great Wind! Now, let me think. What's the next line? 'From the clearing in the pines, Look for the grizzly's jowl.' Papa said Honeysuckle Cottage was built on an old clearing in the pines—but I've never seen a grizzly's jowl."

By this time, the cubs had finished all the windows except the one in Dusty's room. Dusty was hoping to reach it from the inside, but Lucky beat him to it. When Dusty got to his room, there was Lucky sitting on a limb outside the window. The squirrel was making faces and breathing fog on to the freshly cleaned glass! Dusty giggled and went over to thank his friend.

"Hey! Thanks a lot, Lucky," Dusty began, and then he saw something through the glass that he had never noticed before. It was a golden glow that seemed to be coming from somewhere on the other side of the lake.

"That's it!" Dusty shouted! "Great Bear Lake!" The lake was shaped like the head of a giant grizzly bear. Dusty figured the jowl would be right where the glow was coming from.

Without a word, Dusty ran straight for the lake with Lucky following close on his heels. Papa recognized the look of The Fever, so he ran after Dusty and caught up to him just as he was about to jump in the lake.

"Wait a minute there, son!" warned Papa. "You're not thinking straight. If you're so determined to find that treasure you better do it right or you'll end up getting hurt."

Papa borrowed a rowboat and supplies from Grandpa Buzz, and Granny Rose gave Dusty a backpack with a lunch in it. They were finally going treasure hunting!

RISKY JOURNEY

They were only halfway across the lake when The Great Wind started up as suddenly as it had the night before. "We must get to shore quickly!" shouted Papa over the roaring wind.

Papa and Dusty rowed with all their might. The wind blew up huge waves that drenched them and tossed their boat like a toy. Dusty hung on tight, but one tall wave heaved him and all their supplies out of the boat and into the angry water.

Dusty struggled to keep his head above water, but the waves were too strong for him. Once, twice, three times he got pulled under, until at last he had no more air . . . and no more strength left to swim. With pleading eyes, he looked up to his Papa for help as the waves began to drag him down for the last time.

Risking a rescue in these waters was dangerous, but if Papa didn't act now, Dusty would sink into the watery darkness forever.

Without another thought, Papa whispered, "Jesus!" It wasn't a long or fancy prayer but it was from the heart; a prayer from a papa to God, asking for strength to do the impossible.

Then he reached down with heroic strength and wrestled Dusty away from the waters that held him. It was just in time too, because the next wave pitched their boat onto the rocky shore with a *crash!*

LOST GOLDEN HONEY HIVE

Papa gently picked up Dusty's limp body and ran to the nearby shelter of some fallen logs. He shielded Dusty from the wind and whispered loving words to him.

Later, when the winds died down, Papa went to take a look at the boat. It had a large hole in the bottom of it!

Dusty limped over and saw what an awful fix they were in. "Oh, Papa. How will we ever get home?"

Papa thought for a moment, then he simply replied, "God knows."

"But the boat has a hole . . . and we don't have any tools. . . and we're all *alone,*" Dusty added sadly.

Papa admitted, "Part of what you're saying is true. But you're wrong if you think we're alone. God promised that He'd never leave us. As long as God is here, we're never hopeless—no matter how bad things look." It reassured Dusty to hear Papa speak so confidently.

Just then, Dusty felt a tapping in his backpack. He took it off and looked inside. There was Lucky, all scrawny and dripping wet with Granny Rose's lunch all over him. "Lucky! What are you doing in there?" Dusty asked in amazement.

"Don't tell me that you have The Fever, too?" Papa chuckled. Lucky just shrugged his shoulders and grinned. "Well, we've come this far, boys, so we might as well see how this adventure ends. Let's see. I believe we're at 'Top of hill and count to five.'"

Dusty felt like the brave Straight Arrow when, just as the poem foretold, five paces after they reached the top of the hill, his eyes fell upon an incredible sight. There in an enormous twisted oak was a massive Golden Honey Hive!

Dusty and Lucky sprinted for the treasure. Lucky sat on a limb while Dusty pulled off a huge hunk of honeycomb. The honey flowed out of the hive like a golden river and made a puddle on the ground. This hive was loaded with honey! Dusty counted to three, and they both took a taste.

A Change of Heart

"*I-I-ICK! It's bitter!*" hollered Dusty as he tried to spit out the horrible stuff.

Lucky also made a face and spit out the honey. He nibbled on the tree's bark trying to get rid of the taste. But in his haste, he lost his footing and fell right into the middle of the sticky goo. Dusty tried to help, but he pulled too hard. Lucky went flying down the hill like a

bullet and landed tail first in the boat. There he sat with his sticky tail wedged tightly into the hole!

As hard as Papa and Dusty tried, they could not pull him from it. That's when Lucky got an idea. He tapped and chattered until Dusty finally understood. "Oh, I get it! He thinks, if we keep his tail wedged in the hole, we just might be able to use the boat to get home."

"Great idea, Lucky!" Papa congratulated. "That might work!"

Papa and Dusty rowed back across the lake with little Lucky wedged tightly in the bottom of the boat like a cork in a bottle. They got to shore just as the honey was getting mushy.

Grandpa Buzz was there to greet them. He helped them give Lucky one last tug, and with a *"pop"* Lucky was finally free, tail and all!

All the way home, Papa told their story and Grandpa Buzz *"oohed"* in amazement. As Dusty listened, he began to think about the harm his treasure hunting had done. He shuddered when he remembered almost drowning. Then it occurred to him that something could have happened to Lucky or Papa, too. No treasure, not even a *real* Golden Honey treasure, would be worth that! His heart sank, and he began to feel ashamed of himself.

HOME SWEET HOME

From the clearing in the pines, a golden glow of light poured through the windows of home. Mama, Ashley, JJ, and Granny Rose ran out to greet them.

After a welcome home snack of Toasty Teddies, they all joined paws and prayed that night. They thanked God for keeping Papa and Dusty safe, and they

thanked God for their little friend Lucky. Mama tucked Dusty into bed that night as she had ever since he was just a little cubby. She listened as Dusty said his bedtime prayer and then she gave him a hug, a kiss, and a tickle.

"Hugs and kisses, tickles, too . . . are my way of saying, I'll *always* love you!"

"Always?" Dusty questioned with a quiver in his voice.

"Always!" Mama said lovingly.

"Even when a cub has something like, let's say. . . Golden Honey Fever?"

"Even then," she added with a grin and a nod.

"You know what, Mama?" Dusty whispered softly. "I think that's the best treasure of all."

Then she kissed his forehead once more and said goodnight. And Dusty felt all warm inside.

WELCOME HOME TEDDIES

This recipe is a favorite of JJ's. It's "ea*thy* and deli*thith*!" as he would say! A special treat for a warm "welcome home!"

SCRUMPTIOUS STRAWBERRY BUTTER
(Prepare before toasting the Teddies)
- ♥ 1 cup unsalted butter (2 sticks) at room temperature
- ♥ 1/2 cup chopped fresh or frozen strawberries
- ♥ 2 tablespoons powdered sugar

In a small bowl, beat the ingredients with an electric mixer until well blended. The butter will be pink and dotted with bright red bits of strawberry. Pack the butter in a small crock or pretty serving bowl. Spread the butter generously on the Toasty Teddies.

TOASTY TEDDIES
- ♥ Sliced white or whole wheat bread
- ♥ A Teddy Bear cookie cutter (or any shape will do)

Toast your bread, then cut out your "Teddy" shape using a cookie cutter. (Save the bread crusts to feed the birds.) Then spread on your Scrumptious Strawberry Butter. Put them on a cookie sheet and bake at 350° until the butter melts, about 2 or 3 minutes. Using a spatula, place them on a pretty platter and serve them with a smile!

LET'S TALK ABOUT BEARY TALES

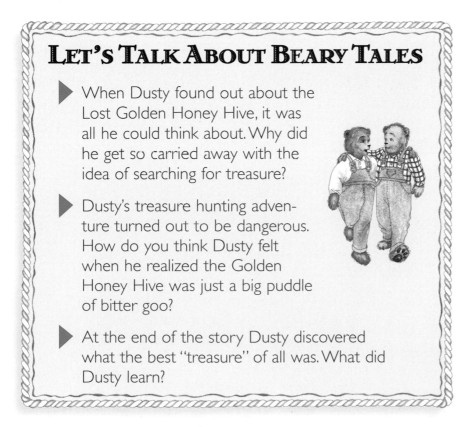

▶ When Dusty found out about the Lost Golden Honey Hive, it was all he could think about. Why did he get so carried away with the idea of searching for treasure?

▶ Dusty's treasure hunting adventure turned out to be dangerous. How do you think Dusty felt when he realized the Golden Honey Hive was just a big puddle of bitter goo?

▶ At the end of the story Dusty discovered what the best "treasure" of all was. What did Dusty learn?

"I will remember the deeds of the Lord;
yes, I will remember your miracles of long ago"
(Psalm 77: 11).

GRANNY'S ATTIC

KEY THOUGHT

Heirlooms are the key that opens the door to memories.
They help us to remember God's faithfulness through the generations.

Late in winter, when the temperature would begin its roller coaster ride toward spring, the silent woods in Maple Country would come to life. Bears would arrive to harvest maple sap and make maple sweets. It was more than just a time to work. The event celebrated the end of the long, sleepy days of winter. There would be fiddle music and dancing, stories and good food. When it was over, there would be enough rich maple syrup and maple candies to last the whole year.

GRANDCUB DAYS

But making maple sugar was hard work so the Mama and Papa bears would go alone. Their cubs would stay with their Grandbears. The Grandbears planned fun things to do and gladly spoiled the cubs. The cubs thought of it as a holiday. They called it Grandcub Days.

This year the Great Wind had ushered in a very harsh winter. Blistering cold and blizzards had kept the cubs indoors far too long. They were really looking forward to the holiday!

When the day finally arrived, they celebrated! It was just warm enough to enjoy playing outdoors, and that's the first place the cubs headed. They made angel bears in the snow. Then Ashley and Dusty made a twisty sled run. It was a thrilling ride. But it was JJ who *accidentally* discovered that it was even more thrilling to slide down by the seat of his pants!

By the time they got to their Grandbears' house, they had color in their cheeks and a sparkle in their eyes. "*Rrring.*" The three cubs stood there beaming as Granny Rose opened the door.

"Hello, Cubcakes! Come on in." They went in and joined Grandpa Buzz at the kitchen table.

"Would you like a little snack?" Granny Rose asked with a grin.

It was a familiar game to the older cubs. They eagerly played along. It began with a stern warning from Granny Rose. "There will be no dessert until you eat your vegetables!"

They happily chirped back, "Oh, yes, Granny Rose. May we please have some vegetables?"

The cubs really didn't care for vegetables. In fact, they thought they tasted pretty yucky. But Granny's vegetables were a completely different matter. They clapped when she brought in a big platter full of them because Granny's vegetables were really delicious Honey Cakes—Honey Cakes shaped like vegetables.

Ashley giggled when she asked Grandpa to please pass the "broccoli." Dusty actually begged for more "onions"! Grandpa Buzz made all sorts of yummy noises as he finished off a big plate of "brussels sprouts." Even JJ pleaded for "More vegetable*th*, plea*the*!"

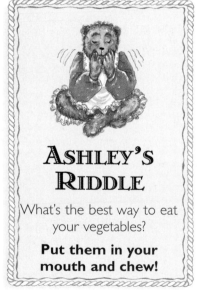

ASHLEY'S RIDDLE

What's the best way to eat your vegetables?

Put them in your mouth and chew!

ATTIC ADVENTURES

Grandpa Buzz and Granny Rose usually announced their plans for the holiday at the kitchen table. When nothing was said, Dusty popped the question, "So what are we going to do?"

Grandpa said, "Oh, I don't know. Granny, why don't we clean out your attic this year?"

"That's an excellent idea!" she heartily agreed.

"Clean out Granny's attic?" the cubs gasped.

This was *not* what they had in mind. They had been stuck indoors all winter. That attic was overflowing with all the things Granny had collected and saved through the years. Cleaning it out could waste their whole day! The cubs began to moan and roll their eyes.

Granny Rose responded with a firm "*Tut-tut!* We can make an adventure out of anything—even cleaning the attic!"

"Give it a try," Grandpa Buzz added with a knowing smile.

The cubs, who had arrived with a skip, now dragged their feet all the way up to the attic.

Dusty opened the creaky old door and they peered into the darkness together. They could only see outlines and shadows. But there was enough light to see that, in places, things were stacked all the way to the ceiling!

"It'*th* gonna take forever!" JJ whined.

"Papa's wagon isn't even big enough to carry away all this *junk!*" Dusty complained.

"Junk?" Now it was Granny's turn to gasp. "You need this adventure even more than I thought. Now follow me, cubs. Grandpa, would you bring the lamp? We're going to need some light in here."

When they reached the center of the room, Granny turned to the cubs. "Let me make one thing perfectly clear. I don't believe in saving *junk!*"

The cubs shrugged their shoulders. It sure looked like junk to them.

"Junk doesn't mean anything to anyone. It's easily thrown away. Nothing in this attic could ever be called meaningless. Why, everything here has a story—a story that means something to the Beary family."

"Even this cup?" Ashley asked. She held up a teacup she found on top of a trunk of old clothes.

"Of course! That teacup belonged to Great Aunt Cora Belle. She was quite an actor, I'll tell you. She starred in 'Little Cubettes.'"

"She did?" Ashley asked with surprise. She'd never known anyone else in her family who liked acting.

"Oh, yes. One day while she was on stage, she won the heart of a certain young bear. He sent her that lovely teacup with a note asking her to tea. They eventually married."

With great interest, Ashley began to organize the things in the trunk. When she got to the bottom, she exclaimed, "It's Cora Belle's costume!"

She tried on the graceful red satin dress and twirled around. Granny Rose looked on admiringly.

While Ashley and Granny Rose worked on the trunk, Grandpa Buzz and the boys cleared away the boxes that blocked the attic window. In no time, the fresh gleam of sunlight once again lit the attic.

The cubs looked around them in amazement. There were colorful old quilts, stacks of dusty books, old-fashioned toys, and all sorts of odd things.

JJ spotted something by the toys that interested him right away. It was a small pouch that held brightly colored glass marbles. "What about thi*th*, Granny?"

"Help me put the toys on the shelf and I'll tell you all about it." she said. "This story begins in Honey Pine Woods, long before there was a Honeysuckle Cottage or a Cub World Toy Store."

JJ could *not* imagine that.

"The Reverend Thaddeus J. Beary was your Great Grandpa Griz's cousin. In a letter, Grandpa Griz told him that there was no church in the woods. Thaddeus felt that God wanted him to start one for them. So, he packed up his family and moved.

"He held services every Sunday at Fern Hollow Chapel. During the week, he would go out into the woods to pray for bears who were sick. One day while he was visiting, he met a young cub named Buster. Even though there was snow on the ground, Buster was not warmly dressed. He didn't even have snow boots! His Ma had sewn flour sacks around his feet to keep them warm."

Granny Rose led JJ to the window and pointed out at the icy snow. "Can you imagine how cold that cub must have been?"

She sat down and snuggled JJ comfortably onto her lap. The cubs and Grandpa Buzz gathered around. They all listened closely as Granny continued.

"Thaddeus could see that Buster was embarrassed about the flour sacks. Buster dug his feet deep into the snow to hide them. Thaddeus pretended not to notice. When he invited Buster to Sunday School, Buster's eyes just lit up! Then Buster looked at his feet and sadly shook his head 'No.'

"Thaddeus knew what he must do. He took the little bit of money they had saved and bought a pair of boots for the cub. When Buster saw them, he hugged Thaddeus. The next Sunday, Buster was there in the front row, wearing his new boots and a big smile.

"Buster gave Thaddeus a special gift, too. He handed him a small pouch. Buster's Ma had made it from the flour sacks. In it were those marbles you found. They were Buster's prized possession."

JJ looked at the marbles. He thought they were the best he had ever seen!

"Little Buster Berryhill gave his heart to Jesus one Sunday. When he grew up, he became a preacher. You know him as the very kind Reverend Berryhill from Fern Hollow Chapel."

The cubs were really surprised.

As Granny spun her stories, the Bearys of long ago became just as real to the cubs as Grandpa Buzz and Granny Rose. Some Bearys had been brave. Others had been afraid. Some were noble. Some were just silly. But each one was special in his or her own way.

They worked on cleaning the attic as Granny told story after story. But it hadn't felt like work at all. They hardly wanted to leave the attic when Granny finally announced it was time for dinner.

Dusty was the last to go. A chill began to creep into the old attic, so he found an old coat to keep him warm. He stood at the window for a moment to watch the sun set behind the Big Log Mountains. The attic was quiet and dark again. He thought, *It has been a good day. A day we will never forget.*

He looked around the attic and smiled. Granny was right. Nothing in this attic was junk.

GRANNY'S STORY

Dusty got to the table just as they were praying for the meal. Grandpa Buzz finished with a loud "Amen!" When he looked up and saw Dusty, his jaw dropped. "Well, what do you know!"

Granny looked to see why Grandpa was so amazed, and exclaimed, "Dusty! You found it!" She sounded relieved.

"What did I find?" Dusty asked, looking puzzled.

"You found *the coat*," she explained. "I thought I had lost it!"

As they ate their dinner, she began to tell them the mystery behind the old coat Dusty had found.

"This story is my most favorite. It begins after your Grandpa and I had been married for quite some time. We always wanted a cub of our own. But we had given up hope that we would ever have one. That's why it was such a wonderful surprise when we found out that we were going to have a little cubby, your Mama Violet.

"We were so excited that we started getting ready right away. Grandpa Buzz worked on the nursery, and I knitted cubby clothes. And every day we asked God to keep our little cubette safe.

"Well, it was early spring and your Grandpa's bee hives needed checking. Sometimes, after a harsh winter, the bees need to be fed a little honey. It keeps them going until the flowers blossom. He didn't want to go, but I assured him we still had at least three more weeks to wait. I told him it wouldn't be right to let the bees starve. So he headed off.

"I tell you what. Let's leave these dishes for later. Bring your cocoa and get comfortable over by the fireplace."

JJ sat on Grandpa Buzz's lap. Teddy Jingles had a warm spot by the fire. Dusty and Ashley each sat cross-legged on a cushion beside Granny's rocker.

"Where was I? Oh, yes!"

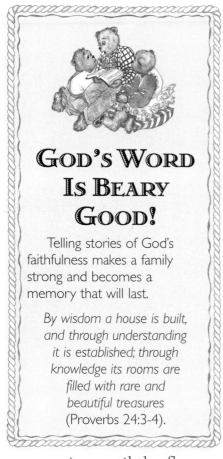

GOD'S WORD IS BEARY GOOD!

Telling stories of God's faithfulness makes a family strong and becomes a memory that will last.

By wisdom a house is built, and through understanding it is established; through knowledge its rooms are filled with rare and beautiful treasures (Proverbs 24:3-4).

MIRACLE IN THE WOODS

"Now, newborn cubs don't know about schedules. They come in God's time. But I didn't know that then. So I was really surprised when I realized that your Mama was coming early. I had planned to stay with Mrs. Appleton when the time came. She knew all about newborn cubs since she had six cubs of her own. So I decided to hike there by myself. I packed a few things and left a note for Grandpa.

"I was about halfway there when I fell. It felt like I had broken my leg. I could go no farther.

"I had told Mrs. Appleton not to expect me for several more weeks, and I didn't know when your Grandpa was due home. Sometimes he'd be gone for days when he was out checking his hives. It could be

days before someone would know I was missing. It started getting dark, and I was really afraid." The cubs knew how scary the woods could be at night. It gave them the chills to think of their Granny Rose out there all by herself.

"After a time, I began to hear the sweetest music. It sounded far away, but I could tell that it was the sweet chords of a harmonica. The tune was a comforting hymn my ma had taught me when I was just a cubette." Grandpa got his fiddle and played while Granny sang the old hymn to the cubs:

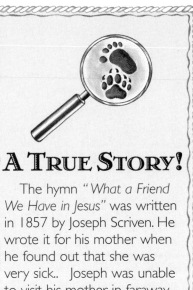

A TRUE STORY!

The hymn *"What a Friend We Have in Jesus"* was written in 1857 by Joseph Scriven. He wrote it for his mother when he found out that she was very sick.. Joseph was unable to visit his mother in faraway Ireland. He wanted to bring comfort to her, so he wrote her the words to this much-loved hymn.

What a Friend we have in Jesus, all our sins and griefs to bear!

What a privilege to carry, everything to God in prayer!

O what peace we often forfeit, O what needless pain we bear,

All because we do not carry everything to God in prayer!

What a friend we have in Jesus, all our sins and griefs to bear,
What a privilege to carry, everything to God in prayer.

"The song reminded me of something. I had forgotten to pray! With tears streaming down my face, I cried out to God.

"A few moments later, that harmonica player showed up. He was a cub

about your age, Dusty. His name was Bo. He said he had heard me crying and came to help.

"He offered to head straight for Mrs. Appleton's, but I asked him to stay with me for a while. I couldn't bear to be left alone again. He gave me something to eat from his backpack. He even gave me his coat and lit a small campfire.

"When I found the harmonica in his pocket, he explained how his ma always sang hymns. He showed me where she had sewn the name of the hymn he had been playing on the inside of his jacket. She had told him that if he ever needed help, it would remind him to pray.

"Soon I started feeling better. My leg still hurt, but I realized that it wasn't time for your Mama to come after all. It was a false alarm.

"So I sent Bo to Mrs. Appleton's place. In a short time both she and Grandpa showed up. You see, Grandpa had come home early. When he saw my note he had rushed over to Mrs. Appleton's to check on me. Since I wasn't there, they guessed something had happened along the way.

"As they helped me home, I told them that I was really thankful that Bo had found me. They gave each other a strange look and then asked me, 'Who's Bo?'

"I said, 'You know, the cub who told you where to find me. He gave me this coat to wear. And, look! This is his harmonica in the pocket.'" Granny's eyes shone with excitement.

Then Grandpa took over the story. "Well, we hadn't seen any cub, and Mrs. Appleton didn't have a neighbor with a cub named Bo."

"How'd you find her?" Dusty wondered.

"I climbed up the tallest tree I could find and spotted the smoke from her campfire." He answered.

Everyone sat in absolute silence.

Then Dusty looked inside the coat. There *"What a Friend We Have in Jesus"* was embroidered, just as Granny had said. And in the pocket he found a silver harmonica.

"We may never really solve the mystery behind the coat. But in my heart, I think that Bo was an angel sent by God," Granny said. "He was the answer to my prayer."

GOING HOME

That night the cubs laid out quilts in front of the fireplace and camped out. They had just drifted off to sleep when they heard music coming from outside. They ran to the window. There Granny Rose, Grandpa Buzz, Mama,

and Papa were laughing and square dancing in the snow by the silvery light of the moon. Mama and Papa were finally home, and the wagon was filled with maple sweets!

When the cubs unpacked back at Honeysuckle Cottage, they found surprises in their bags.

Ashley squealed when she found Cora Belle's teacup. JJ shouted, "Yippee!" when he found the bag of marbles. And Dusty was amazed to find the harmonica tucked in his bag. Each gift came with a handwritten note. It read "A Treasure from Granny's Attic!"

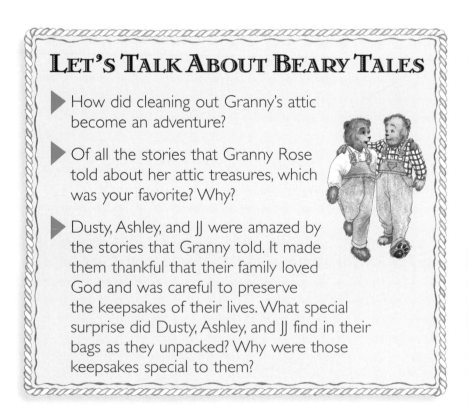

Dusty sat on the edge of his bed and tried blowing through the harmonica. It would take practice to play well, but he already knew the first song he wanted to learn. He began to play, "What a friend we have in Jesus. . . ."

LET'S TALK ABOUT BEARY TALES

▶ How did cleaning out Granny's attic become an adventure?

▶ Of all the stories that Granny Rose told about her attic treasures, which was your favorite? Why?

▶ Dusty, Ashley, and JJ were amazed by the stories that Granny told. It made them thankful that their family loved God and was careful to preserve the keepsakes of their lives. What special surprise did Dusty, Ashley, and JJ find in their bags as they unpacked? Why were those keepsakes special to them?

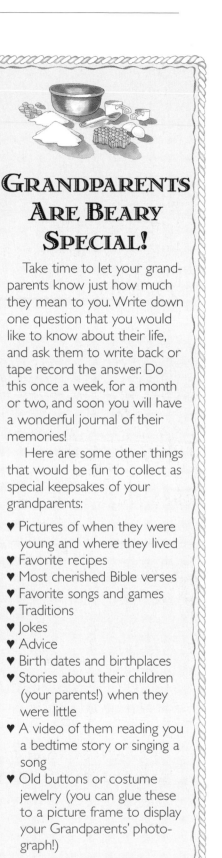

GRANDPARENTS ARE BEARY SPECIAL!

Take time to let your grandparents know just how much they mean to you. Write down one question that you would like to know about their life, and ask them to write back or tape record the answer. Do this once a week, for a month or two, and soon you will have a wonderful journal of their memories!

Here are some other things that would be fun to collect as special keepsakes of your grandparents:

♥ Pictures of when they were young and where they lived
♥ Favorite recipes
♥ Most cherished Bible verses
♥ Favorite songs and games
♥ Traditions
♥ Jokes
♥ Advice
♥ Birth dates and birthplaces
♥ Stories about their children (your parents!) when they were little
♥ A video of them reading you a bedtime story or singing a song
♥ Old buttons or costume jewelry (you can glue these to a picture frame to display your Grandparents' photograph!)

It would also be fun to decorate a special box for the keepsakes you collect.

"Whatever you do, work at it with all your heart"
(Colossians 3:23).

GOING ON A BEARY HUNT

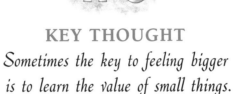

KEY THOUGHT

*Sometimes the key to feeling bigger
is to learn the value of small things.*

ome cubs call their younger cubbies a bother. But Dusty loved being JJ's big brother. He would mess up JJ's fur and cross his eyes just to hear him giggle with delight. And he liked doing little things for him.

One time JJ admired a teddy bear in the window of Cub World Toy Store. Dusty swept floors at the store for a month to earn enough money to buy it for JJ. (That floppy teddy became JJ's very own Teddy Jingles!)

JJ loved and admired Dusty. When he was first born, he couldn't sleep a wink unless Dusty was curled up beside him. And though most cubs say "Honey" first, JJ's first word was "Du*thty*." In fact, the older JJ got, the more he wanted to be just like Dusty. He said everything Dusty said until he sounded like an echo.

But even cubs who really love each other quarrel sometimes.

CUBBY TROUBLE!

This quarrel started over dominos. Dusty had won every game, and JJ was getting tired of it. When it looked like Dusty was about to win again, JJ threw Teddy Jingles at the dominos. They scattered everywhere.

JJ claimed, "Teddy did it!" but Dusty knew better. He was so mad that he called JJ a "*cubby*." It may not sound like a bad name, but no growing cub wants to be called a cubby, even if he acts like one.

ASHLEY'S RIDDLE

Why did the little bear cub put honey under his pillow?

He wanted to have "sweet dreams"!

JJ stomped down the hall into Ashley's room. He hoped that she'd be on his side. But Ashley didn't want to talk about "a silly domino game," as she put it. She suggested that they play house, instead. She didn't bother to wait for JJ's answer. She just went searching for a bonnet for him to wear. Well, there was no way JJ was going to play "Ashley's precious cubby," even if it meant he got fed plenty of hot cocoa and cookies!

He escaped to his nursery room and sulked. "Du*th*ty call*th* me a cubby. Ashley trea*tth* me like one. I even have to *th*leep in the nur*th*ery! It'*th* ju*th*t not fair! I'm not a CUBBY!"

PICKING BRAMBLEBERRIES

The next morning the sun was bright, and the sweet fruity smell of spring was in the air. It had been a long time since the long, cold days of winter. Everything in the woods was alive with color. It was Brambleberry season!

Unfortunately, Grandpa Buzz and Papa couldn't help out with the berry picking today. A raccoon with a sweet tooth had damaged some of their best hives while trying to steal honey. They were going to have to spend the day making repairs.

The Brambleberry harvest would not be easy without Papa and Grandpa. So they decided to split up the tasks.

Mama volunteered to go to town for supplies. Ashley gathered up all the canning jars and lids. Granny Rose would boil the jars and get the kitchen ready. And everyone agreed that Dusty should gather the Brambleberries. He'd gone into the backwoods with Doc to harvest roots and herbs lots of times, so he knew just where to go.

Mama looked the list over and finished with, "It's settled, then. We'll each do our chores and meet back here at noon to can the berries. Then, tonight we'll celebrate with Brambleberry Cobbler! Does everyone know what to do?"

JJ cleared his throat. "What about me, guy*th*?"

Mama thought for a moment. "I think you'd better go with Dusty. A cub should never go into the backwoods alone."

Any other time JJ would have jumped at the chance to be Dusty's partner. But JJ didn't feel the same since his quarrel with Dusty. Dusty thought he was a cubby! JJ had heard it with his very own ears. Just the idea of it made him feel awful!

TROUBLE IN THE BACKWOODS

All the way up Windy Trail, JJ thought about his cubby trouble. He figured that all Mama really wanted was for Dusty to cubby-sit him. "Why can't I have a real chore like everyone el*the*? I don't need a cubby-*th*itter!" he said to himself.

He dragged farther and farther behind until Dusty had to stop to let him catch up.

"Hurry up, JJ, or we won't get back to Honeysuckle Cottage in time," Dusty urged. Then he noticed that JJ's shoe was untied. Dusty knelt down and started to tie it for him. Any other time, JJ would have realized that Dusty was just trying to be nice. But not today.

JJ put his hands on his hips and scolded Dusty, "Don't treat me like a cubby, Du*th*ty. I can tie my own *th*oe!"

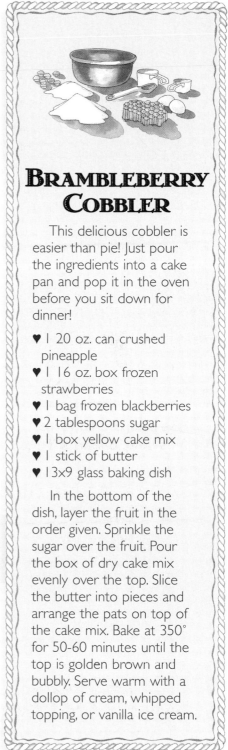

BRAMBLEBERRY COBBLER

This delicious cobbler is easier than pie! Just pour the ingredients into a cake pan and pop it in the oven before you sit down for dinner!

- ♥ 1 20 oz. can crushed pineapple
- ♥ 1 16 oz. box frozen strawberries
- ♥ 1 bag frozen blackberries
- ♥ 2 tablespoons sugar
- ♥ 1 box yellow cake mix
- ♥ 1 stick of butter
- ♥ 1 3x9 glass baking dish

In the bottom of the dish, layer the fruit in the order given. Sprinkle the sugar over the fruit. Pour the box of dry cake mix evenly over the top. Slice the butter into pieces and arrange the pats on top of the cake mix. Bake at 350° for 50-60 minutes until the top is golden brown and bubbly. Serve warm with a dollop of cream, whipped topping, or vanilla ice cream.

GOD'S WORD IS BEARY GOOD

Dusty realized that what he said to JJ was unkind. He remembered what the Bible said about our words.

Reckless words pierce like a sword, but the tongue of the wise brings healing (Proverbs 12:18).

They walked quietly along the path for a while. Then Dusty said what he should have said the day before. "JJ? I'm sorry I called you a . . . cubby. I didn't mean it. I was just mad about the dominos."

"Are you *thure?*" JJ questioned sadly.

"I'm sure," Dusty said. He reached down and put his arm around JJ's shoulders. But JJ shuffled along as if something was still bothering him.

"If I'm not a cubby, then how come I never get *important* chore*th?*" JJ finally questioned.

"What's an important chore?" Dusty asked.

"It'*th* one a grown-up cub doe*th.* Like you get to go to town by your*thelf* to pick up thing*th* for Mama. And Papa let*th* you chop wood. You get to do important chore*th!*"

JJ kicked a rock with the toe of his boot and said, "All I ever get to do are the cubby chore*th. Thtupid thtuff* like taking out the tra*th* or picking up kindling wood."

Dusty led him to a shady spot and sat him down. "It's true. I do chores that you're not allowed to do. But that's now. When I was your age I didn't get to do them either."

"You didn't?" JJ said.

"Oh, no. And there are still a few chores that I'm not allowed to do. I'm not allowed to go away on the honey harvest yet. And I'm not allowed to drive Papa's wagon to town by myself. There's a right time for everything. And your chores are just perfect for you right now," Dusty reassured him. "Besides, whatever gave you the idea that your chores are not important? Have you ever thought about what would happen if no one did your chores?"

JJ shook his head.

"If no one took out the trash, the cottage would soon get so smelly we wouldn't like living there. And there certainly wouldn't be any Honey Cakes without kindling wood!"

"Really?" JJ gasped. "Why?"

"Kindling wood is what gets the fire going. It's impossible to make a good fire without it. And without a good fire, Mama couldn't bake your Honey Cakes. "I'd say your chores are *very* important. Wouldn't you?"

JJ had to agree.

54

"But how about today?" JJ questioned. "I think Mama really ju*tht* wanted you to cubby-*thit* me. Right?"

"Oh, no. Mama was right to send you along. Cubs should never go into the backwoods alone. You should always take a hiking buddy with you. If one cub gets in trouble the other one can help out. I was counting on you to be my partner." Dusty hesitated. ". . . but I understand if you don't want to be partners with me, after what I said and all."

JJ thought about it. Then he gave Dusty a friendly slug on the arm and said, "*Aaaw* come on. Let'*th* get going, partner."

THE RUMBLE

The Brambleberry patch was loaded with berries. In no time, the cubs had their pails and their tummies full.

They were laughing and racing each other back down the path, when suddenly they felt a strange shaking under their feet. Dusty knew to look out for falling rocks in the backwoods. A dangerous flood of rocks and dirt could break away from the cliffs and crush them.

Dusty quickly searched for a safe place to hide. He spotted a small cave just a few steps in front of them. He grabbed JJ's hand and ran for it.

The rumble was louder than thunder!

Even inside the cave, dirt pelted them. It felt like hundreds of little needle pricks. They covered their faces the best they could, but clouds of dust billowed up and began to sting their eyes and choke them. They coughed and hacked until their throats were sore.

When the rumble died down, the cubs stood in total darkness. A wall of rubble

CAVES ARE AWESOME

Caves are large hollow spaces inside the earth. Most caves have winding passages that trail for miles! The ceilings sometimes have strangely shaped rock formations that look like icicles hanging down. They are called stalactites. Many caves even have lakes or waterfalls and rivers flowing through them.

Animals that live in caves include raccoons, birds, bats, crickets, and bears. Cave exploring can be very interesting but also very dangerous! The safest way to explore a cave is by visiting one that provides tours for groups of people.

completely blocked the entrance to the cave. They were trapped!

JJ began to cry. He didn't care if someone thought he was a cubby now. He was scared.

Dusty reached out for JJ and pulled him close. He put his arms around him, hugged him tight, and began to pray.

DUSTY'S PRAYER

Dear Heavenly Father, I know You are here. We are not alone. Your words in the Bible tell us that You are always ready to help us in times of trouble. Lord, we are in trouble! Please send someone to help JJ and me. Thank You for keeping us safe from the falling rocks, and thank You for Your promise to never leave us! In Jesus' Name, Amen.

HUNTING FOR THE BEARY CUBS

It hadn't taken long for Mama and Granny Rose to realize that something was wrong. They sent Ashley to go tell Doc. (He was the leader of the Woodland Search and Rescue Team when Grandpa Buzz was not available.)

Doc sent Mrs. Nuthatch to Honeysuckle Cottage. She was to set up a First Aid Station just in case someone was hurt and prepare food for the team. She was a helpful sort of bear, with a good listening ear and a knack for making a warm cup of tea.

Mrs. Nuthatch was followed by Reverend Berryhill, his wife Emma, and their oldest cubette, Gracie. They brought along boxes full of supplies that had been donated by the Bearys' friends at Fern Hollow Chapel.

It was really something to see how the whole town rallied together in an emergency.

A "CUBBY" SAVES THE DAY!

Dusty and JJ were not sure how long they had been trapped in the cave. They had lost track of time in the darkness. They worked together to start clearing a path through the rubble. When their paws became too raw from scooping away at the dirt, they took turns using

Dusty's scout knife to dig. It seemed like hours and yet they still hadn't broken through to the outside.

Then there was one last earth-shattering rumble. But this time, a tiny ray of light broke through a small hole at the entrance to the cave. It was such a relief!

The sight of daylight gave Dusty an idea. He tried to push his way through the hole but it was no use. "I'm too big to fit through," he finally admitted.

But JJ's eyes lit up. "I'm *th*maller than you are. Maybe thi*th* i*th* a chore that I could do."

Dusty examined the small hole carefully, then he looked at JJ and smiled. "I'd say this chore is perfect for you."

JJ took off his belt and shoes. He figured it might help him fit through the hole easier. Then he looked down at Teddy Jingles. He didn't like to be without his old friend. But when he thought about Dusty waiting in that dark cave all by himself, he made up his mind.

"Here, Du*th*ty. You keep Teddy Jingle*th* with you," he said bravely. Dusty smiled and gratefully accepted the gift.

JJ squirmed, and twisted, and heaved until he finally pushed himself out into the fading sunlight. Then he marched straight over to the pathway and did just as Mama had taught him. She said if they were lost or needed help they should "Hug a tree!" So that's what he did.

When the Woodland Search and Rescue Team finally arrived, they found JJ hugging that tree. After JJ told them what happened, Doc congratulated him for his good sense. Then JJ proudly led the team to the cave and showed them just where to dig.

With JJ's help they were able to get Dusty out in no time. In just a few hours everyone was safely back at Honeysuckle Cottage. The cubs even remembered to bring home the Brambleberries.

They arrived home to a feast of Mrs. Nuthatch's special Jingle Bear Pancakes. (She named them after JJ's Teddy Jingles.) Then as a special treat, she tied jingle bells to the cubs' forks. JJ giggled and clapped his paws when he saw them. He ate four helpings for himself and two helpings for Teddy Jingles.

JINGLE BEAR PANCAKE PARTY

Make plans to have a Jingle Bear Pancake Party just like Mrs. Nuthatch had for Dusty and JJ! You'll have a bear-rel of fun!

Here are some ideas:

♥ Decorate the center of your table with teddy bears. You can put them in a basket tied with a big bow or in a small toy wagon filled with hay. Add some red apples and pine trimmings for color.

♥ For fun, tie jingle bells to your forks with red ribbon. (You can get the bells at a craft store.)

♥ Make teddy bear shaped place cards, giving everyone a bear name! (Heather-bear, etc.).

♥ Whip up your favorite pancake recipe. Then, with a serving spoon, slowly drizzle the batter on a hot griddle to form two small ears, an inch apart, then a larger dollop for the face. When bubbles form and pop it's time to flip the bearcake. Serve with happy music, maple syrup, and fresh berries!

A NEW ROOM FOR JJ

Not long after that, Papa announced, "JJ, it's time you moved out of the nursery."

They were welcome words to JJ. But when Mama suggested that JJ share Ashley's room, you should have seen the look on his face. Poor JJ. He imagined spending the rest of his cubhood dressed in a cubby's bonnet. He plunked his elbows onto the table so his paws propped up his sad little chin.

Then Dusty whispered something to Mama and Papa. They both heartily agreed. Papa told JJ, "Just leave the matter in our hands, JJ. You'll have a room in no time!"

Mama hung a sheet across the kitchen and said, "No peeking." And JJ didn't peek, even though the noise of hammering and sawing continued for days.

When they finished they led JJ into the kitchen. There in the far corner was a sturdy new pine cupboard. JJ couldn't help but feel disappointed. Did they really think he should sleep in a cupboard? But it only took a moment for his disappointment to turn to joy.

Dusty knocked firmly on the wall three times. With that, the cupboard door popped open to reveal a secret stairway! The stairway led to a loft that Papa and Dusty had built over the kitchen.

First, JJ noticed that he had a birds-eye view of the kitchen from up there. He could look down and watch Mama cook. He could even see inside the cooking pots on the stove. And all the delicious kitchen smells drifted up to his room and made it smell all buttery and sweet.

Then he noticed an iron pulley on the wall. Hanging from it was a rope with a bucket tied to the end. Dusty said it was an easy way to get things upstairs. And Papa gave the cubs a ride in it. They said it was more fun than the roller coaster ride at the Honey Pine Woods Country Fair.

It was a wonderful room, and it had all been Dusty's idea!

That night JJ invited Dusty to camp out in his new room. Mama made a soft bed out of old Indian blankets for them. Then she rang a bell and told them to haul up the bucket. When they did, they found fresh Brambleberry Cobbler inside!

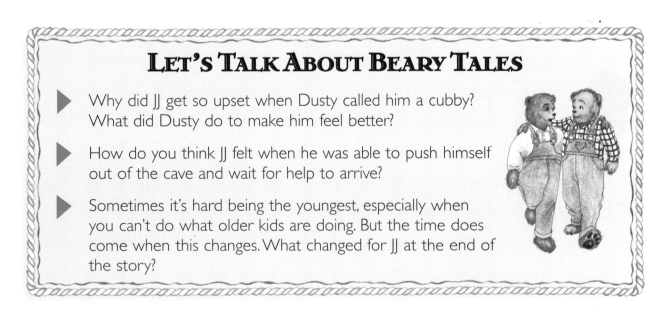

After they had eaten their fill, the cubs stretched out on the soft blankets. JJ laid on his back and looked up at the ceiling with his paws folded behind his head. He said,"Du*th*ty?"

Dusty rolled over to face him. "Yes?"

"Thank*th* for explaining to me about my chore*th*."

"You're welcome," Dusty replied.

JJ yawned and said in a sleepy voice, "Did you know that Mama'*th* baking Honey Cake*th* tomorrow?"

"Really?" Dusty rolled onto his back and stared at the ceiling. "I love Mama's Honey Cakes."

"They're the be*th*t!" JJ agreed. "I gue*th* I better get up early and collect the kindling wood."

Dusty smiled. "That's a good idea," he said. He knew JJ didn't feel like a cubby anymore, and it made him glad.

Dusty curled up next to JJ, just as he had when JJ was a cubby, and went to sleep. He knew they would always be friends.

LET'S TALK ABOUT BEARY TALES

▶ Why did JJ get so upset when Dusty called him a cubby? What did Dusty do to make him feel better?

▶ How do you think JJ felt when he was able to push himself out of the cave and wait for help to arrive?

▶ Sometimes it's hard being the youngest, especially when you can't do what older kids are doing. But the time does come when this changes. What changed for JJ at the end of the story?

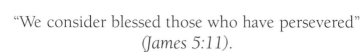

"We consider blessed those who have persevered"
(James 5:11).

THE FIRST HONEY HARVEST

KEY THOUGHT

Anyone can give up when things get hard.
Sometimes the key to succeeding is to keep on trying.

It was a lazy summer day in the woods. Dusty and Rusty strolled out to the end of the creaky old boat dock. They sat down and dipped their bare feet into the cool blue water of Great Bear Lake. They had gone out there to eat their ice cream and to skip rocks across the water.

Rusty studied the pile of rocks that sat between them. He picked up one that was about the size of an acorn. Squinting, he aimed for a spot near the buoy that marked the edge of the swimming area. With a quick motion, he sent the rock sailing. It skipped across the top of the water five times before it finally sank.

"You're a lucky cub," Rusty said.

Then Dusty took his turn, as Rusty looked on and talked.

"Imagine spending a week in the backwoods surrounded by nothing but honey! I wish I could go."

Actually, Dusty would have been relieved to stay home and let Rusty go on the Honey Harvest in his place. It's not that

he disliked honey, mind you. But there was something that he was not looking forward to . . . the bees!

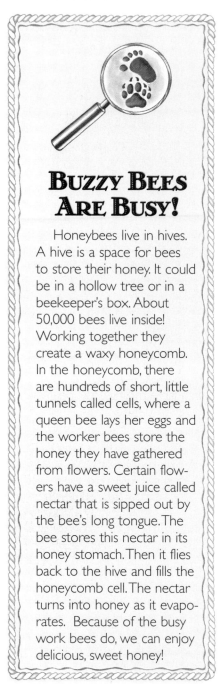

BUZZY BEES ARE BUSY!

Honeybees live in hives. A hive is a space for bees to store their honey. It could be in a hollow tree or in a beekeeper's box. About 50,000 bees live inside! Working together they create a waxy honeycomb. In the honeycomb, there are hundreds of short, little tunnels called cells, where a queen bee lays her eggs and the worker bees store the honey they have gathered from flowers. Certain flowers have a sweet juice called nectar that is sipped out by the bee's long tongue. The bee stores this nectar in its honey stomach. Then it flies back to the hive and fills the honeycomb cell. The nectar turns into honey as it evaporates. Because of the busy work bees do, we can enjoy delicious, sweet honey!

Bears weren't supposed to be afraid of bees. Mama said he didn't need to be afraid. She said God had given bears a thick fur coat to help protect them from bee stings. But he just couldn't help it. He was really afraid of getting stung.

Of course, that whole experience with Mr. McGruder and the hanging beehive had made things even worse. He had made those bees so mad that they chased him all the way to Strawberry Creek. He had to hide under water to get away from them.

That day, he discovered there is at least one place where a cub's fur does him no good—right on the tip of the nose. Some angry bees had seen his nose sticking up out of the water and had stung it again and again. It became so red and swollen that he looked like Rudolph the Red-Nosed Reindeer!

There was no doubt about it. Dusty was *very* afraid of bees. He wouldn't admit it, of course, especially to Rusty. So he kept his thoughts to himself.

PRIZE-WINNING HONEY

Beekeeping was a proud Beary family tradition. The Bearys had owned a hundred acres of prime bee territory in the backwoods since Great Grandpa Griz's time. Each summer they made the big trip into the backwoods to harvest honey. Every cub looked forward to the day when they would finally be allowed to go. Every cub, that is, except for Dusty.

This was going to be Dusty's very first Honey Harvest. Grandpa Buzz and Papa were going to teach him the secrets of their success. Their bees produced the finest honey in the woods. In fact, their honey won blue ribbons at the Honey Pine Woods Country Fair almost every year!

LEAVING FOR THE BACKWOODS

Dusty's big day finally arrived. Mama prepared a huge breakfast of Cocoa Cubbies in honor of the occasion. All through the meal, Ashley and JJ chattered away about how excited they were for Dusty. They could hardly wait until it was their turn to go on the harvest.

Even Mama couldn't contain her excitement. "Why, I remember my first harvest as if it was yesterday . . . the sweet smell of honey, the joyful humming of the bees. I was so excited that I couldn't eat my breakfast, either," she said as she looked at Dusty's uneaten plate of food.

But Dusty's lack of hunger had nothing to do with being excited. The more he thought about those bees, the more he worried. And the more he worried, the sicker he felt.

Meanwhile, Grandpa Buzz and Papa were busy loading supplies onto the honey wagon. Buttercup, Grandpa's favorite horse, was all ready to go. She looked silly wearing Granny Rose's old straw gardening hat on her head, but Grandpa insisted that she liked wearing it. She nibbled on some flowers while she patiently waited for them to finish.

Buttercup always went on the Honey Harvest. She had been a fine horse in her day. Her mane was all streaked with gray now, and she didn't move as fast as she used to, but Grandpa said none of those things mattered. Buttercup had been a faithful old gal, and her good old-fashioned "horse sense" had come in handy a time or two. Grandpa always brought her along.

"Everything's packed and we're ready to go," Grandpa Buzz cheerfully announced as he finally stepped into the wagon and took up the reins. Papa settled in next to him, and Dusty took his place in the bed of the wagon.

Grandpa Buzz flicked Buttercup's reigns and clicked his tongue. "*Tchk, Tchk!* Easy does it, girl."

COCOA CUBBIES

Mama always bakes Cocoa Cubbies for her cubs' special occasions. And Dusty's first Honey Harvest certainly was something special!

- ♥ 2/3 cup soft butter
- ♥ 1 cup sugar
- ♥ 2 eggs
- ♥ 2 teaspoons vanilla
- ♥ 2 1/2 cups flour
- ♥ 1/2 teaspoon baking soda
- ♥ 1/4 teaspoon salt
- ♥ 1/2 cup unsweetened cocoa

Preheat the oven to 350°. In a large mixing bowl beat the butter, sugar, eggs, and vanilla. Add the dry ingredients, and mix until well blended. Wrap the dough in plastic wrap and refrigerate about an hour.

Once the dough is firm, shape it into small balls. Place these cocoa balls onto an ungreased cookie sheet. Press your thumb in the middle of the ball to make a "paw print." With the small rounded end of a wooden spoon gently poke in 5 little toes. Bake 8 minutes. After baking, poke the toes in one more time.

Buttercup snorted and jerked the wagon to life. With each plodding step she took, Dusty nervously watched Honeysuckle Cottage grow smaller and smaller. He knew he was leaving the safety of home behind. He would soon come face to face with those dreaded bees.

SETTING UP CAMP

They reached the backwoods territory by afternoon. After they unloaded the wagon and set up camp, even Dusty had worked up a grizzly-sized appetite. Luckily, there were plenty of fish in the clear mountain streams. They were able to catch all they could eat before nightfall.

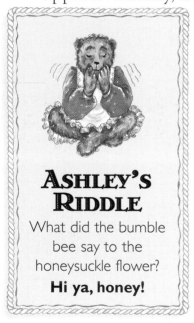

ASHLEY'S RIDDLE

What did the bumble bee say to the honeysuckle flower?

Hi ya, honey!

"*Ahhhh.* Fresh trout. There's nothing like it!" Papa said as he rubbed his furry round belly and stretched his toes out toward the dancing light of the fire.

Dusty had to agree. The meal tasted delicious.

Grandpa Buzz brought out his fiddle and began to play "The Crawdad Song." Papa joined him on the banjo. It was such a happy tune, Dusty even tried to play along on his harmonica.

Then Papa pulled out a bag of marshmallows. They told jokes and laughed while they roasted the marshmallows over the campfire.

It was so peaceful in the backwoods. Dusty was finally beginning to relax. That night he fell asleep without even thinking about the scary bees.

THE BIG DAY!

Dusty woke the next morning to the wonderful smell of hot cocoa and frying bacon. He smiled and took in a deep breath.

"Mornin', Grandpa. Mornin', Papa," Dusty called brightly.

Grandpa noticed Dusty's good mood. "I see that life in the backwoods

agrees with you, Dusty. I know something else that's going to agree with you. Honey straight from the hive. You're gonna love it!"

"Honey? Hive? Oh, no!" Dusty hid his head in his paws. "How could I have forgotten about the bees?"

"What's the matter, son?" Papa asked as he walked over to Dusty. "You looked fine a moment ago. Now you look a little . . . well . . . green!"

"I don't feel well," Dusty moaned. And it was true. His belly was growling at the thought of those bees.

Both Grandpa and Papa looked Dusty over, but they couldn't seem to figure it out. They asked, "What kind of strange illness is this? It came on so suddenly!"

"We'd better not take a chance, Dusty. Now, I know you're counting on going with us today, but I think you better stay right here. We'll leave you with Buttercup, and you try to get some rest. We'll see you back here at dinnertime," Papa said.

Dusty tried to look disappointed, but he felt relieved. He was so relieved that he spent the day swimming, hiking, and feeding Buttercup wild flowers. Grandpa and Papa returned to find Dusty looking much better.

A Dose of Honey for Dusty

The next morning Dusty awoke in worse shape than he had been in the morning before. His belly didn't hurt, but *that's* what was bothering him. He knew if he didn't have a bellyache, Papa would make him go for sure.

"How's your belly this morning, son?" Papa asked when he saw that Dusty was awake.

Dusty couldn't lie. "It's not hurting, Papa . . . but maybe I should stay here another day, just to make sure."

Papa suspected that Dusty's problem had something to do with the harvest. "Maybe a dose of honey would perk you up?" he suggested. It was an unfair trick—no cub could turn down a dose of honey.

When Dusty happily agreed, Papa said, "Good! Then get dressed and come along. We'll give you a big dose of honey from our hives!"

Dusty had been outsmarted. He would *have* to go on the Honey Harvest now. Dusty got dressed and walked stiffly over to where Grandpa and Papa stood

waiting for him. One look at him and they both started to chuckle. Dusty had put on four shirts and every pair of overalls that he had. He had on so many layers of clothes that he could hardly walk! And even though it was summer, he wore a knit ski mask over his face!

"Nice outfit, Dusty." Papa chuckled. "But, don't you think you're dressed a bit too warmly for honey harvesting?"

"Oh, no, Papa. I'll be just fine," Dusty said trying to look calm and casual.

It didn't take long to hike to the first hive. They were just a few yards away when Dusty heard it. The bees were "humming," as Mama would say. To Dusty it sounded more like a round of machine-gun fire.

He hid behind Grandpa and Papa as they began to take out their gear. They planned to use smoke to calm the bees, but it was Dusty who needed help being calm. The more he thought about bees, the more he began to shake and sweat. Soon he was breathing so fast that his head was swimming.

Now, as it happened, one honey bee seemed particularly curious about Dusty. Perhaps it had never seen a bear so bundled up before. The bee landed squarely on the end of Dusty's nose and looked him straight in the eye. Dusty stood still. Then he lost control. He swatted at the bee with his paws and began screaming at the top of his lungs. He screamed all the way back to the campsite.

Papa and Grandpa looked at each other in stunned silence.

DUSTY FACES HIS FEAR

Dusty wanted to crawl into a cave and hide. He kept thinking, *I'm supposed to be grown up, but I acted sillier than a cubby! How can I face Papa and Grandpa now? What will they say? After all, who ever heard of a bear being scared of a tiny bee?*

Buttercup looked at him with her kind brown eyes. When Dusty saw her, he put his paws around her neck and sobbed until her mane was wet.

Buttercup let out a low whinny. Dusty wiped his eyes and gave her a faint grin. He knew she was trying to make him feel better.

Buttercup's nose gently nudged Dusty. She was trying to get him to go somewhere. Dusty sniffed. "What's up, old girl? Where are we going?"

She just kept on nudging him—all the way back to where Grandpa and Papa were working.

"Stop! I don't want to go back there," Dusty kept telling her. But Buttercup just kept walking and gently nudging Dusty along.

"Ah! There you are, Dusty," Grandpa called out with a smile. "I was beginning to wonder if Buttercup had lost her knack." But she hadn't. She had used her good old-fashioned "horse sense" to bring Dusty right back where he belonged.

Papa put his arm around Dusty's shoulder and gave him a squeeze. "You should have said something, Dusty. I would have understood. I could have helped you."

"I was too ashamed, Papa," Dusty admitted sadly.

"Son, there's no shame in being afraid. Everyone is afraid sometimes. But it's a real shame to let your fears get the best of you. You have to find a way to face your fears, or they'll keep you from doing all sorts of great things."

"But how? Every time I even hear those bees I start shaking."

Then he heard Grandpa begin to play softly on his fiddle. "How about a little music to help you forget the buzzing, Dusty?" Music as sweet as honey began to cover up the sound of the bees. Dusty began to relax.

Papa taught Dusty how to move calmly and slowly around the bees. He stayed right beside Dusty and gently showed him just what to do. Papa even put a drop of honey on a stump so Dusty could get a close-up look at a honeybee. Dusty had never seen such a long tongue. The bee used it like a straw to suck up the honey. Bees didn't look so scary when Papa was by his side.

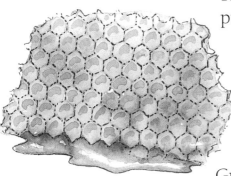

Then Papa handed Dusty a piece of honeycomb. It was beautiful. Each cell was perfectly formed and filled to the brim with golden honey. It looked like the stained-glass window at Fern Hollow Chapel. And it tasted even better than Grandpa had said it would!

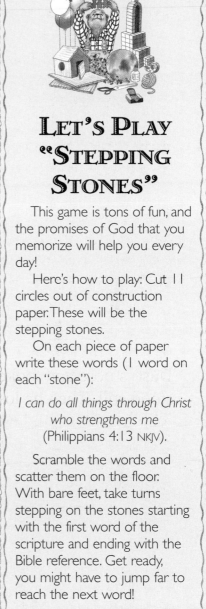

LET'S PLAY "STEPPING STONES"

This game is tons of fun, and the promises of God that you memorize will help you every day!

Here's how to play: Cut 11 circles out of construction paper. These will be the stepping stones.

On each piece of paper write these words (1 word on each "stone"):

I can do all things through Christ who strengthens me (Philippians 4:13 NKJV).

Scramble the words and scatter them on the floor. With bare feet, take turns stepping on the stones starting with the first word of the scripture and ending with the Bible reference. Get ready, you might have to jump far to reach the next word!

Try this game with other scriptures. You can cover each stone with clear plastic adhesive shelving paper, so you can use them again and again.

Remember, you can get over your fears just like Dusty did, step by step!

Each day after that, Grandpa played his fiddle while Papa showed Dusty how to harvest the honey. When they were done, Dusty found that honey harvesting wasn't nearly as scary as he had thought it would be.

GIVING THANKS

The last night around the campfire, everyone was much quieter than they had been the first night. They had worked long and hard, and they were tired. But it was a good kind of tired. And it had been worth the effort. The honey wagon was filled with their best crop of honey yet.

Dusty laid on his sleeping bag and looked up at the stars. He rubbed a small spot on the end of his nose. He had gotten stung once. But it hadn't hurt much.

Papa poked at the fire with a stick and then added a few more logs. He looked over at Dusty and said, "Tell me, Dusty, what have you learned?"

Dusty scratched his head and thought about it. "I learned that things didn't get better until I faced my fear of those bees. And now I'm really glad that I did. It wasn't so scary once you showed me what to do, Papa. And beekeeping can be very rewarding. I mean, just look at all the honey we've got!"

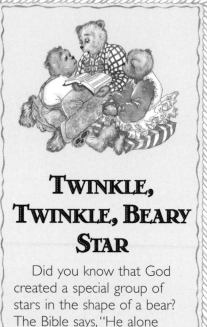

TWINKLE, TWINKLE, BEARY STAR

Did you know that God created a special group of stars in the shape of a bear? The Bible says, "He alone stretches out the heavens and treads on the waves of the sea. He is the Maker of the *Bear* and Orion, the Pleiades and the constellations of the south" (Job 9:8-9).

A group of stars is called a constellation. There are two Bear constellations. The Big Dipper is part of the Great Bear constellation and the Little Dipper is part of the Little Bear constellation. Next time you look up into the night sky, see if you can see that twinkle, twinkle, Beary star!

Papa grinned. "You've learned some valuable lessons, Dusty. Now there's just one more lesson that you must learn before we leave."

Papa pointed toward the stars that glittered in the night sky. He used his finger to draw an imaginary line between the stars, one by one. When he was done, Dusty could see the outline of a bear.

"Every creature on earth has its faults," Papa explained to Dusty. "For the bear? Well, we must be careful not to become full of pride, thinking that it's by our own strength that we survive. We must always remember that it is God who makes us strong. And it is God who made the bees and flowers that we depend on for our honey. So when you look at this bear in the night sky, remember that God takes care of your needs. And then, remember to say thanks."

The eyes of all look to you and you give them food at the proper time. Psalm 145:15

Grandpa Buzz opened up the Bible and read Psalm 145:15. *"The eyes of all look to you, and you give them their food at the proper time."* Then they closed their eyes and thanked God for another wonderful harvest of honey.

Dusty would go on many Honey Harvests in the years that followed. But he never learned quite as much as he did on that very first one.

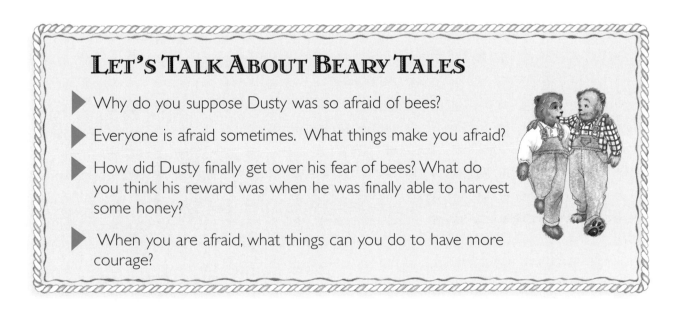

LET'S TALK ABOUT BEARY TALES

▶ Why do you suppose Dusty was so afraid of bees?

▶ Everyone is afraid sometimes. What things make you afraid?

▶ How did Dusty finally get over his fear of bees? What do you think his reward was when he was finally able to harvest some honey?

▶ When you are afraid, what things can you do to have more courage?

"TELL ME WHY THE STARS DO SHINE, TELL ME WHY THE IVY TWINES, TELL ME WHY THE SKY'S SO BLUE, AND I WILL TELL YOU JUST WHY I LOVE YOU. BECAUSE GOD MADE THE STARS TO SHINE, BECAUSE GOD MADE THE IVY TWINE, BECAUSE GOD MADE THE SKY SO BLUE, BECAUSE GOD MADE YOU, THAT'S WHY I LOVE YOU."

"Come before him with thankful hearts.
Let us sing him psalms of praise"
(*Psalm 95:2 TLB*).

HOEDOWN IN HONEY PINE WOODS

KEY THOUGHT
*The key to becoming thankful
is to begin counting your blessings.*

The Beary family cellar was filled to the brim with all the food they had grown in their garden. Onions with their tops braided together hung drying, along with bunches of wild flowers, above the doorway. Bright orange pumpkins were lined up neatly beside barrels of potatoes and carrots. On the shelves were rows of preserves and jars of rich amber-colored honey that glowed like jewels when the light touched them.

From the look of that cellar, anyone could see it had been a very good year for the Bearys!

The only fall project left was cleaning out Grandpa's barn. The cubs were supposed to clean up Buttercup's stall, rake out the hayloft, and then put a thick layer of fresh hay everywhere. Afterwards, they could play in the barn whenever they wanted to. And they loved playing barn games!

The cubs worked together the rest of the day and finished the barn in no time. First they played Barn Swing. Grandpa Buzz had tied a long rope to one of the rafters. The cubs liked to swing on the rope like Tarzan. They'd get

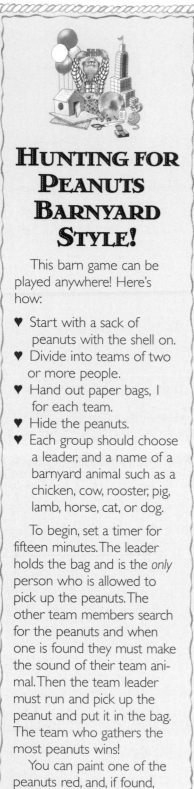
swinging really high, then they'd let go and fall into a huge mound of hay. It was great fun!

When JJ landed he'd sink so far down he'd disappear from sight. Dusty and Ashley had just rescued him from the hay, when JJ spotted a set of eyes peeking out from behind the barn door.

JJ laughingly called out, "Ya wanna *th*wing?"

The cub stepped out into the light. "Can't. Gotta finish my chores," she answered.

They scrambled down from the hayloft. Dusty made the introductions while JJ stuck out his paw, "Ni*the* to meet you!" he squeaked, as friendly as can be.

"I'm Molly, Molly Brown," she said as she reached out to shake JJ's paw. "I just moved here with my pa."

"We're going to have a picnic and then play in the barn again tomorrow. Would you like to come?" Ashley asked.

"I'd like that!" Molly replied, grinning from ear to ear.

MOLLY'S LUNCH

The cubs spread one of Mama's colorful quilts under the shade tree beside the barn. Dusty laid out their lunch. They had made Toasty Teddy Sandwiches with extra honey. Granny Rose had squeezed fresh lemonade, and Mama had baked a batch of Honey Cakes for dessert. It was the cubs' favorite picnic lunch.

They had just prayed when Molly arrived. Ashley greeted her first, "Hi, Molly! You're just in time."

Molly sat down on the quilt next to Ashley. She whistled cheerfully as she began unwrapping her lunch. But Molly's lunch wasn't anything like the cubs' lunch. Molly had only a few crusts of dry bread and a wild root from the woods. Ashley was the first to notice, but soon they were all staring at Molly's lunch.

But Molly didn't seem to be bothered by her lunch at all. She folded her paws and prayed as sincerely as if she were thanking God for a honey feast!

Dusty looked at the huge helping of Honey Cake on his plate. He wasn't feeling very hungry anymore. "Molly? Would you like some of my Honey Cake?" he offered.

Molly looked at the cake and gave Dusty a big smile. "Yes. Thanks!" she said.

She looked more pleased than Dusty had when he came home with his first Bearball card. She took one tiny bite, then she carefully wrapped the rest of the cake in the cloth napkin that she had brought her lunch in.

JJ scratched his head. "Aren't you hungry, Molly?" he asked.

Ashley was afraid that JJ's question might embarrass Molly, so she whispered, "JJ, be quiet."

Molly didn't seem embarrassed, though. She rubbed her belly and licked her lips. "There is *nothing* better than Honey Cake. . . unless, it's *sharing* that yummy Honey Cake with my pa!" she said with a giggle.

Molly was the most unusual cub they'd ever met. She just seemed to accept things that other cubs grumbled about. Her pa may not have a lot to give her, but he'd given her the most important thing of all—love. And Molly had more than enough of that. So, in spite of everything, she was a happy cub.

COUNT YOUR BLESSINGS

Sunday was the beginning of the Honey Pine Woods Thanksgiving celebration. Each fall, after the harvest, the community set aside time to thank God for their blessings. The celebration began with Sunday services at Fern Hollow Chapel.

Reverend Berryhill led the congregation in a joyful chorus of "Count Your Blessings." It was the topic of his message that morning. At the end, he handed out pencils and paper hearts and asked everyone to write down their blessings.

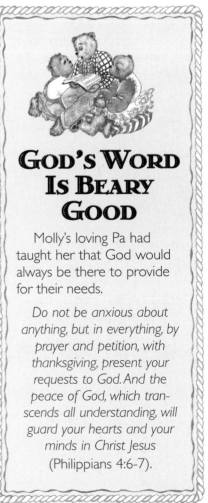

GOD'S WORD IS BEARY GOOD

Molly's loving Pa had taught her that God would always be there to provide for their needs.

Do not be anxious about anything, but in everything, by prayer and petition, with thanksgiving, present your requests to God. And the peace of God, which transcends all understanding, will guard your hearts and your minds in Christ Jesus (Philippians 4:6-7).

Papa, Mama, Dusty, Ashley, and JJ each took turns writing their blessings on the paper hearts. They watched as each blessing made their stack grow taller.

Then Ashley poked Dusty in the ribs and pointed to the front pew. There sat Molly and her pa. They lived in a little shack behind Timberlake Lumberyard. Molly's pa hadn't worked much lately. Yet Molly and her pa were smiling and holding a stack of hearts as tall as the Bearys'!

NEIGHBORS HELPING NEIGHBORS

Gracie Berryhill and Dusty talked while everyone tied the hearts onto the bare limbs of the huge quaking aspen tree in the churchyard.

"There's got to be something we can do to help the Browns," Gracie said. "I don't see how they'll last through the winter. I'm afraid they'll starve."

The thought had been bothering Dusty, too. He had even talked to Mama about it. She had told him about the early days in Honey Pine Woods. The pioneers survived the winter on very little, but not without the help of their neighbors. It gave Dusty an idea.

With Gracie and the cubs' help, Dusty started something he called "Neighbors Helping Neighbors." The idea was to share their extra food with their neighbors. Some families had more than enough potatoes; others had corn to spare. The Bearys had a bumper crop of honey. Everyone had something to share. Even Molly and her pa had extra wild herbs. And everyone would be able to trade their surplus for things they really needed.

Reverend Berryhill thought it was a wonderful idea! In fact, he suggested they collect clothes and shoes for cubs who needed them during the cold winter months, too.

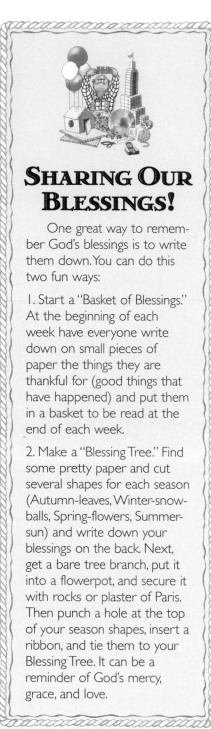

SHARING OUR BLESSINGS!

One great way to remember God's blessings is to write them down. You can do this two fun ways:

1. Start a "Basket of Blessings." At the beginning of each week have everyone write down on small pieces of paper the things they are thankful for (good things that have happened) and put them in a basket to be read at the end of each week.

2. Make a "Blessing Tree." Find some pretty paper and cut several shapes for each season (Autumn-leaves, Winter-snowballs, Spring-flowers, Summer-sun) and write down your blessings on the back. Next, get a bare tree branch, put it into a flowerpot, and secure it with rocks or plaster of Paris. Then punch a hole at the top of your season shapes, insert a ribbon, and tie them to your Blessing Tree. It can be a reminder of God's mercy, grace, and love.

Getting Ready

Now, the Hoedown was the last big community gathering before winter. It started with a huge potluck dinner and games at Sugar Pine Park. Later, the Bearys would pull out their instruments for an evening of good old-fashioned country music. It was the best part of Thanksgiving week! Every year, family and friends drove in from miles around for the Hoedown. The cubs thought it was the perfect time for their "Neighbors Helping Neighbors" plan. If they worked really hard, they figured they could have everything ready for the Hoedown on Saturday.

Word about the cubs' idea spread like wild fire. Everyone was excited and wanted to help. Mr. Bookman suggested they set everything up in the schoolhouse. Mama, Papa, and the Berryhills offered to pick up the donations. Mrs. Nuthatch volunteered to help the cubs sort through the clothes and other gifts. By the end of the week, the little schoolhouse was filled to the rafters!

A BEARY FUNNY JOKE!

Why are false teeth and the stars alike?

They both come out at night!

The Bearys' Hillbilly Band

All week long, the Bearys returned home from the schoolhouse tired from working. Then they spent the evenings getting ready for the Hoedown. There was sewing and baking to do. And, of course, the band had to practice.

Grandpa led the band with his fiddle. Papa played along on the banjo. The two of them would play and then tell a few jokes. This year Dusty was going to join them on his harmonica. He had been practicing every day. Now he could play almost every song.

Mama and Granny Rose led the sing-along time. They had always sung duets together but this year they would be singing as a trio. Ashley had a strong, clear voice, so they invited her to join them.

JJ hadn't discovered his talent yet. He was feeling a bit left out, until Papa remembered an instrument he had once played as a cub. He borrowed Granny Rose's washboard and a few of Mama's thimbles. With the thimbles on his fingers, JJ could make that washboard sing! It added a cheerful rattle to the music that JJ loved!

TIME FOR A HOEDOWN

WHAT'S A HOEDOWN?

A hoedown was what a farmer did when he finished a long season of hard work. He would say, "It's time to put the *hoe down* and gather friends together for food and fun!" (A hoe is a longhandled tool with a flat blade, used to break up the dirt or dig weeds.) Everyone would bring a dish of delicious homemade food: fried chicken, corn, potato salad, fresh fruit, rolls, and lots of cakes, pies, and cookies!

After this hearty supper, they would push back their chairs and begin the square dance. Everyone joined in the fun—from children to grandmas and grandpas! There would be fiddles, banjos, mandolins, and guitars. It was a good time to visit and sing favorite old songs with family and friends!

There was excitement in the air. It was Saturday—the day of the Hoedown! Wagons loaded down with happy bears and cubs rolled along the old dirt path that led to Sugar Pine Park. They began unloading baskets of blankets, toys, and delicious homemade treats!

Reverend Berryhill got everything started. He stood on a stump and raised his hands to the sky. Everyone quieted down. Then every bear from the tiniest cubby to the oldest Granny bowed their head and repeated the Thanksgiving blessing.

Father God, You created every berry, nut, and tree. You created my family and friends, and You created me. You're the God of the Honey Harvest and all that is good, true, and loving. For all these things and more, help us to be truly grateful. Amen!

There was a delightful buzz of activity as everyone loaded up their plates with food. Mama's sister Daisy had come with her family. Daisy had brought her homemade honey graham crackers —they were a big hit. JJ liked them so much that he filled his pockets with them. A trail of cracker crumbs spilled out of his pockets as he ran and played with the other cubs.

THE SCHOOLHOUSE BLESSING

Dusty and Gracie met Molly over by the crock of spiced cider. They told her to close her eyes, and they led her down the path to the little red schoolhouse. When she opened her eyes, her mouth fell open. "In my whole life, I've never seen so much food!" she said.

Dusty told her, "You can borrow our wagon to take your supplies home. I think there's just about anything you need in here."

"And look, we saved this box of clothes just for you," Gracie added. "We think they're your size. But Dusty's Granny Rose will help you fix them up so they'll fit just right."

Molly began dancing around the room and singing, "Count Your Blessings," the song she had learned at Reverend Berryhill's Thanksgiving service.

"By the time I finish counting all these blessings, I'll be an old granny!" she giggled.

That afternoon, one by one, bears made their way over to the schoolhouse and marveled at the incredible sight! They each took those things that they needed to fill their pantry for the winter. By the end of the day the room was bare. Everything had been handed out.

The Bearys and the Berryhills, Mr. Bookman, and Mrs. Nuthatch looked at the empty room. They knew no bear or cubby would go hungry this winter. It made them feel good and, indeed, the whole town was proud of what they had done.

STRIKE UP THE BAND!

The sun began to set and everyone cleared out what was left of the picnic. Rusty had been on the winning Bearball team. Doc had won at pig calling. (He said "Pig Latin" was his specialty.) And Ashley surprised them all by winning the pie eating contest!

Jake Brown, Molly's pa, had volunteered to decorate for the Hoedown. Lanterns were strung from one end of the park to the other. When they were all lit it was a sight more dazzling than fireworks! They danced in the breeze like overgrown fireflies.

"He must have borrowed every lantern in town," Mama commented with delight.

Everyone took their places and the Bearys' Hillbilly Band began to play. They started out with "Bear Paw

HOMEMADE HONEY GRAHAM CRACKERS

This recipe comes from Sylvester Graham. In 1794 he invented the Graham cracker because he wanted to eat foods that were good for his body and would taste good too. This yummy honey cracker is a favorite of the Beary family, especially JJ!

- ♥ 3 cups whole wheat flour
- ♥ 1 teaspoon baking powder
- ♥ 1 teaspoon baking soda
- ♥ 1/2 teaspoon salt
- ♥ 1/4 cup honey
- ♥ 1/2 stick softened butter
- ♥ 1/2 cup yogurt
- ♥ 1 cup brown sugar
- ♥ 2 teaspoons vanilla

Combine and mix all of the ingredients until well blended. Knead the dough into a ball. Put it between 2 sheets of wax paper and flatten with a rolling pin to 1/4" thick (you may want to divide the dough in half and do one half first). Peel the top sheet of wax paper off and flip the dough onto a floured cutting board. Take off the other sheet of wax paper. Cut the dough into 2-1/2" squares. Transfer the squares onto a greased cookie sheet with a metal spatula. With a fork dot a few holes in each square. Bake at 350° for 10 minutes.

Polka." Then Grandpa played "Turkey in the Straw" on his fiddle, while Papa began calling the square dance.

"Bees in the honey hive, Busy as you please, Bow to your partner, Scratch those fleas. Now, 'Round the world, And back again, Do-se-do, And peck like a hen."

Everyone linked arms, walked in circles, and added little jig steps here and there. They had loads of fun! Even the cubbies danced.

"Honey Cakes in the pan, Sweet as you please, Promenade, Then bend those knees."

Aunt Daisy joined Mama, Granny Rose, and Ashley as they led the sing-along. They did all the old favorites. They sang cowbear songs like "Git Along, Little Doggies" and "Home on the Range." And silly songs like "Oh, Susanna!" By the time they got to "Hush, Little Baby" all the cubbies were sound asleep. It had been a good day, but it was getting late. It was time to head home.

GOOD NIGHT

The Bearys waved good-bye to their friends and gave Aunt Daisy and her family one last hug before they left. After all, Thanksgiving wasn't just a time to thank God for the *things* He provided. It also reminded them to thank God for friends and family.

Granny Rose and Grandpa Buzz followed Mama, Papa, and the cubs home in their wagon. They gathered out on the front porch of Honeysuckle Cottage. They felt tired but happy. It had been a wonderful Thanksgiving week and the best Hoedown ever!

JJ laid his head in Mama's lap, and she began to lovingly stroke the fur on his fuzzy little head. Dusty and Ashley relaxed against Papa's big, broad shoulders. Granny Rose and Grandpa Buzz rocked slowly back and forth in the old porch rocking chairs.

Far above the towering peaks of The Big Log Mountains, a sea of twinkling stars lit the night. Their message flashed across the heavens. . . . "The Lord will provide." And every living thing seemed to be at rest.

Then Mama and Granny Rose began to sing quietly into the stillness. Their

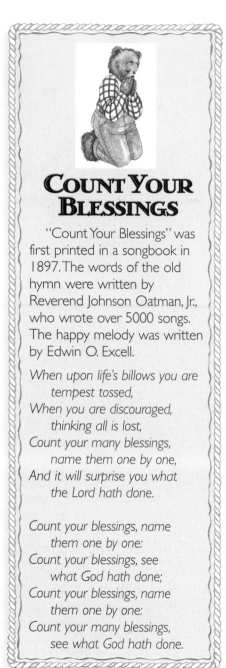

COUNT YOUR BLESSINGS

"Count Your Blessings" was first printed in a songbook in 1897. The words of the old hymn were written by Reverend Johnson Oatman, Jr., who wrote over 5000 songs. The happy melody was written by Edwin O. Excell.

*When upon life's billows you are
    tempest tossed,
When you are discouraged,
    thinking all is lost,
Count your many blessings,
    name them one by one,
And it will surprise you what
    the Lord hath done.*

*Count your blessings, name
    them one by one:
Count your blessings, see
    what God hath done;
Count your blessings, name
    them one by one:
Count your many blessings,
    see what God hath done.*

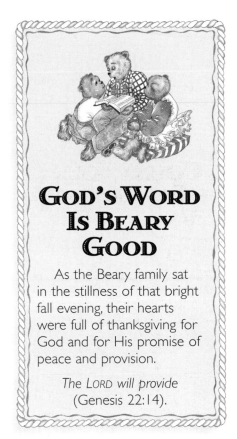

voices blended together in harmony as sweet as golden honey. It was a song that had soothed fussy cubbies for generations. It was Dusty's favorite bedtime song. They sang:

Tell me why the stars do shine,
Tell me why the ivy twines,
Tell me why the sky's so blue,
And I will tell you just why I love you.
Because God made the stars to shine,
Because God made the ivy twine.
Because God made the sky so blue,
Because God made you, that's why I love you.

GOD'S WORD IS BEARY GOOD

As the Beary family sat in the stillness of that bright fall evening, their hearts were full of thanksgiving for God and for His promise of peace and provision.

The LORD will provide (Genesis 22:14).

And Dusty drifted peacefully off to sleep.

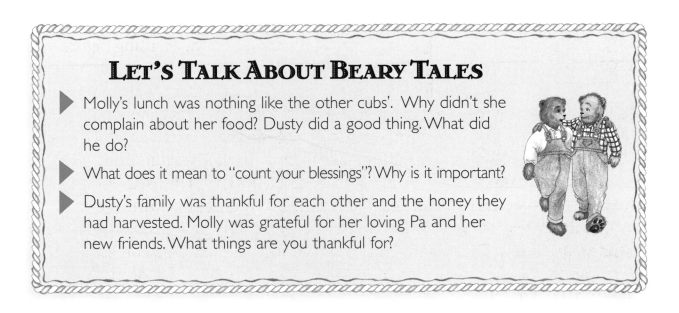

LET'S TALK ABOUT BEARY TALES

▶ Molly's lunch was nothing like the other cubs'. Why didn't she complain about her food? Dusty did a good thing. What did he do?

▶ What does it mean to "count your blessings"? Why is it important?

▶ Dusty's family was thankful for each other and the honey they had harvested. Molly was grateful for her loving Pa and her new friends. What things are you thankful for?

Dear Friends,

   The Bearys have great family adventures! Here are a few ideas to help make these Beary Tales an adventure for your family, too.

♥ **Family Story Time:** Recapture the joy of this old-fashioned pastime. Read a whole chapter or break it up into several smaller readings. Whether you have just a few minutes or a whole evening, it's really rewarding. To make things interesting, take turns reading, or assign parts and read the stories like a play.

♥ **Get Involved:** Try the recipes, activities, and songs with your children. When you finish the book, have your own Thanksgiving Hoedown picnic. Learn one of the Bearys Hillbilly Band songs. Then try to imagine what Papa's silly square dances would look like.

♥ **Talk, Talk, Talk:** These stories are meant to get you talking. The discussion questions and "key thoughts" are great conversation starters. And look for opportunities to share your own experiences. Does the story in "Granny's Attic" remind you of a time when God answered one of your prayers? Talk about it. Then pray about something specific with your children and, when God answers, they'll have a story to pass on to their children. Or, if you want a great keepsake, write down your responses to the discussion questions and save them.

♥ **Children Learn What They Live:** Think of your life as an adventure! Look for ordinary situations in your life that teach lessons like the ones you've read about. Try writing your own real-life adventure tale. Most of all, let your children see you living out the values that you think are important, and have fun!

Teach them to your children, talking about them when you sit at home and when you walk along the road, when you lie down and when you get up (Deuteronomy 11:19).

Wishing You Many Happy Adventures,
Ruthann and Linda